THE WRECKER

DAVID SKINNER

Scholastic Inc.

New York   Toronto   London   Auckland   Sydney

ISBN 0-590-93976-9

Copyright © 1995 by David Skinner.
All rights reserved. Published by Scholastic Inc., 555 Broadway,
New York, NY 10012, by arrangement with Simon & Schuster.

12 11 10 9 8 7 6 5 4 3 2 1   6 7 8 9/9 0 1/0

Printed in the U.S.A.   40

First Scholastic printing, September 1996

For the boy

We wanted to wreck Jeffrey Pratt. That was Theo's word for it. Wreck. We didn't want him hurt, we didn't want him dead, we didn't even care if he got expelled from William Tecumseh Sherman Junior High. We simply wanted Jeffrey Pratt *destroyed*.

Like, take the kid and —

Shatter his mind.

Burst his soul.

Wreck the kid, once and for all.

On my fourth day at Sherman, Theo came right smack up to me and said, "You're Michael, right?" He said it to me like I was in trouble. But I wasn't in trouble. How could I have been? Heck, I hadn't even *done* anything. I was just standing there waiting for first bell, avoiding everyone and everything, keeping to myself, you know, just the new kid in school...and new kids never want trouble, not with anyone, not on their fourth day, no, not ever. So like I was completely innocent, which I completely *was*, I muttered, "Uh, yes."

Theo looked me over. "You'll do."

Carefully I asked, "Do for what?"

He said, "I'm Theo. I don't need a friend. I can be your friend if you want. Lots of people seem to need friends. Normal people. I'm not normal. You look kind of normal. I can be your friend. That's okay. You seem cool. You better be. But I don't need a friend, I need an ally, and if you won't be my ally, then you can just go join the rest of *them*," he pointed at the other kids, "and be boring stupid normal all you want. They'll be your friends, okay? But you'll be my ally, right? Yes or no? Nod once for yes if you forgot how to talk. Do you ever forget how to talk? I hope you never forget how to nod."

Have you ever been pushed, chest first, by a rushing crowd into a concrete pole? I have. It's like your lungs just stop. Like you forget how to breathe. In front of Theo that day I forgot how to breathe, how to talk, how to nod. But he didn't care. I didn't even have to say yes. Theo had chosen me to be his ally, and that was that.

He said, "Okay then, we're allies," and went away, and I was alone where I'd been, waiting for school to start.

At first I was afraid Theo really meant that stuff about being allies. I didn't want to be Theo's ally. I didn't want to be anyone's ally. Besides, Theo was just plain *scary*, and I liked my life unscary.

Don't get me wrong. I did like my life to be unscary, and most of the time I was meek, but don't think I was some sort of tranquil lamb. I mean, think about this. After first bell I went straight to my first-hour class—history with Mr. Fusillade. And what was I doing that morning as I sat in Mr. Fusillade's room? Working? Studying? Meditating? No, I was drawing a Martian storm trooper, an interplanetary killer in full body armor. That armor was gouged with Martian battle phrases like *Krekko narkana* and *Xevokki aei*, which I had made up to mean *Onward to Glory!* and *Death to the Enemy Hordes!* The helmet, dark visor and all, had a snarling metallic demon on top. The trooper carried a laser rifle; slung across his chest were hundreds of spiky grenades. I had his foot crushing the head of a captured spy from Neptune. The entire scene was done up on loose-leaf in the busiest, blackest ink. I had started it the day before, during English class, as Ms. Gasperwit had puffed on about something.

So—still think I might have been a lamb? I, who drew pictures of nastiness and ignored my teachers while I drew?

Now, boys who draw Martian storm troopers (and at the same time ignore their teachers) are not so unusual. They're not necessarily bad, either. The point I'm trying to make is that even though Theo scared me, he and I did become allies. We were the same kind of misfit, you see. We each had what you could call an *unquiet spirit*. Mine mostly just inflated my daydreams; Theo's, on the other hand, always boiled and made him *move*.

But I'm getting ahead of myself.

I was in Mr. Fusillade's room, drawing. Class hadn't started yet. Only a couple of other kids were in there as well. All the rest of my classmates, like most of the kids at

Sherman, were spending that time before first hour cruising the hall—girls with boys, boys with girls, kids with kids in chattering clumps. I was glad to be away from them all.

Theo found me there.

He kind of snuck up on me, or maybe I was just too involved to notice him coming. Anyhow, he had a chance to look at my drawing before he spoke, and so when he did speak he asked, "What's *Krekko narkana*?"

He startled me, of course. I didn't answer him right away. I hesitated. "What's *Krekko narkana*?" he asked again, and I said, "Nothing, really."

"Well, then you shouldn't write it down." He sat in the desk in front of mine. He faced me. "A soldier, right? That looks like a laser rifle to me. That's how I'd draw a laser rifle. Who's that he's stepping on?"

"Um. A spy."

"Doesn't look human."

"He's not."

"Is he from Mars?"

"No. The soldier's from Mars. The spy's from Neptune."

"Ah." The bell for first hour rang. "Look," he said, "we've got to meet after school. Plan things. Figure things out. I need to show you something. We're allies, so you can see it, but you can't tell anyone. Good allies keep secrets. You're my ally because I could tell you'd keep a secret. You'd never talk to anybody. Right?"

The room was filling up. Mr. Fusillade was leaning back in his chair, saying hi to everyone who came in. Some kids he greeted by making a gun out of his hand and cheerfully *shooting* them. That's how he was. Theo, meanwhile, though he seemed unhurried, was going to be late for his class. There was no time to argue with him. Arguing would have done no good in any event, even if I'd wanted to argue. So I just shrugged like I meant to say, "Okay, I'll go, I'll keep your secret." Theo accepted my shrug. He got up and left.

Theo was right about one thing. I never talked to anybody. I would keep his secret. So long as I knew Theo, so long as we were allies, I never once mentioned the junkpile to anyone.

Sherman was a small school, you know. The building was just a one-story rectangle, and there was only one hall. Turn four corners and you'd be back where you started. It was easy to bump into almost anybody and even easier to find someone. Even if I had wanted to avoid Theo, I couldn't have.

He found me on the way to Mr. Bembo's room. Pressing close, he said, "Don't forget. After school. I need to show you. Okay? Did you forget? Don't, okay?"

Before I could reply, someone behind us cracked, "Look, the girls are kissing." Theo pulled back from me and tensed. Both of us stopped walking. We were right outside Mr. Bembo's door. I turned. It was some kid I didn't know. He circled around in front of us. His eyes were glassy. He squinted, trying to place my face. "You're that new kid," he said. I nodded slowly, not sure what was up. "You're going to Bimbo's right now?" I knew he meant Bembo. I nodded. Theo was breathing evenly. The kid sniffed at me. "Thought so. Dead frogs." I had no idea what he meant. He said, "I should smash you." Now I tensed, too. Then the kid said to Theo, "So, sassy, haven't seen you in a while." Theo glared at him. The kid slugged Theo, threw his fist into Theo's stomach, snarled "You little fag," and went away.

Theo didn't quite double over. He bent like a balsa board, half snapped. His face was red and I could tell it hurt.

There weren't any teachers nearby. We were even right in front of the faculty lounge. The door was open. I could clearly see the magazines and coffee mugs and, in the back, the extra ditto machine. But no teachers.

It had all happened too fast anyhow. The kid was long gone. I didn't know what to do. I asked Theo if he was okay. He said no. I thought I should straighten him, unbreak him. But I was afraid to. When I moved my hand to help, he shrank from me. His face was still red and a little wet too. After a moment Theo went on to his class.

And you know what? Once Theo was gone and I was alone, I realized that I wanted to kill that kid with the glassy eyes. At the time I was surprised by my reaction. But now I'm not so surprised. I know what I was like then.

Like, *Death to the Enemy Hordes*.

The kid was Jeffrey Pratt.

He had been bullying Theo for a month. I had missed the beginning of it (since my family moved into town in early October), but back in September Theo had carried his books like a girl—you know, against his chest, instead of at his side—and he did that just because he had a lot of books and it was easier to carry them that way; but for Jeffrey it was the worst sort of sissiness and a perfect excuse to start in on Theo.

At first Jeffrey's bullying was pretty basic, calling names and all, but then it got really bad. Theo, you see, had this great set of colored pencils. They were for an art assignment. They even had a nice box, a box so nice that

Theo didn't want to wreck it by putting his name on the outside. So he put his name on the inside. One day Jeffrey stole the box of pencils. Jeffrey could be that way, like some little brat. Theo was infuriated. He wanted his pencils back so much that he wasn't thinking straight. He told Mrs. Stencil, the art teacher, that the pencils were his. Jeffrey of course said they were *his*. He got mad at being called a thief and made Theo out to be a troublemaker. But then Theo told Mrs. Stencil, "My name's in the box!" He grabbed the box from Jeffrey and opened it up, and there it was, Theo's name. Jeffrey went devil-red and Mrs. Stencil punished him.

After that, Jeffrey punished Theo.

He slugged Theo all the time. Theo didn't tell. He thought he had been a fool to tell on Jeffrey before—and in a way he had been—and he just didn't want to make it worse. Complaining to anyone would have made Theo seem like a tattletale, even more of a sissy—or, as Jeffrey stupidly put it, a sassy.

So Theo put up with Jeffrey's attacks.

It's not like he could've reasoned with Jeffrey. Bullies are bullies. I mean, Jeffrey didn't even know who *I* was and right away he insulted me, pretending I smelled like dead frogs. That shows, too, how bullies will use any way to put you down.

The dead frogs had nothing to do with me. They had to do with Mr. Bembo. Yes, I was in Mr. Bembo's class, but the whole thing had happened the year before, when I wasn't even going to Sherman. In the spring Mr. Bembo's class had started a project to study the growth of frogs. The kids were supposed to feed the frogs, and sure they fed them, but because Mr. Bembo had given bad instructions the kids fed the frogs *wrong*, and early on the frogs died. Mr. Bembo had wanted the project to last for a few weeks; with five little green corpses on his hands he had to change things around a bit. Now the class was going to study the *decay* of frogs. Every day the kids inspected the frogs and made this simple observation: "They've rotted more today." With rot came stink. The stink got on the room, on Mr. Bembo, and on the kids, and pretty soon the kids were recognized all over school as "the ones who have the dead frogs."

When the project was over, Mr. Bembo said, "Kids, just imagine how those dead frogs, if they had been in the wild, would have fed the slugs and flies and scavengers, and eventually the soil itself. Imagine!" Then Mr. Bembo dumped out the tray of frogs and opened a window to clear the air.

I know I didn't smell like anything, least of all frogs, yet Jeffrey made his two-bit insult and even threatened me, too. But what can you expect? It didn't help that I was with Theo. Maybe, in Jeffrey's eyes, I was Theo's friend. I was fair game.

I saw Theo later in Mr. Shoe's class. We both had Mr. Shoe for math. So, yes, even before Theo made me his ally, I kind of knew who Theo was. After all, I sat behind him— my last name is Wilson, his is Vee—and yet until he made me his ally, Theo never said a thing to me, in class or out.

Now he was silent again. He didn't even look at me. It was because of the run-in with Jeffrey, or so I guessed. Theo was subdued. It was like before, I mean before we'd met. I wasn't sure if I should say something. I said nothing.

Class began. Todd and Robby started acting up; pretty soon they were driving Mr. Shoe nuts. "C'mon, guys," Mr. Shoe said, "I'm warning you," but Todd and Robby didn't care, and after a while neither did Mr. Shoe. He ignored them and tried his best to get on with his lesson.

That was the first year of teaching for Mr. Shoe. You could tell it was tough on him. He didn't make much of a boss, and whenever he had to tell us kids to "listen up" or "quiet down," he seemed uncomfortable. He was kind of wishy-washy.

Sometimes, for just a few moments he would lose his

temper. Anger looked very strange on him. In fact, none of us ever much took his anger seriously. That was part of his problem, I guess. He wasn't believable. Some teachers, when they're angry, dredge up hell for us kids. Not Mr. Shoe. His heart wasn't in it.

Sometimes he would write some of us up, but whenever he did that he merely seemed desperate, and none of us were very scared of the principal anyhow. I suppose our class was a bit cocky. We were definitely rude. Sometimes I had to feel sorry for Mr. Shoe; he seemed so beaten down.

Later on when just he and I were talking, Mr. Shoe admitted that he wasn't always doing what a teacher should. What bothered him most of all is that he often lost track of us. He really didn't know how each of us was doing, how each of us was getting on. Even in October he still confused some of the kids. "Which one is Lori?" he asked me, and I said the one with the long hair. "Oh," he said, "so the curly-headed one is Melissa." I said yeah.

Of course Mr. Shoe never confused *Theo* with anyone. Theo made himself too obvious. You see, Theo was always jumping ahead of Mr. Shoe. Mr. Shoe could be doing this problem or that, and every time, before he could finish, Theo broke in and gave the solution. Theo wasn't smug about it. He gave the solution only because he knew it and had to let it out.

Theo was smart that way.

And every time Theo interrupted him, Mr. Shoe would stay as calm and as nice as ever and say, "Yes, Theo, you're right. Now let me finish." Theo's interruptions could frustrate Mr. Shoe, but Mr. Shoe never got mad at Theo. Of course he never got properly mad at *any* of us, and besides I think he kind of, but only kind of, liked Theo.

Today, however, Theo didn't interrupt Mr. Shoe, not even once. Like I said, Theo was subdued.

At one point one of the kids, I think it was Lori, couldn't tell Mr. Shoe whether 2 went into 544 or not. Mr. Shoe asked if she knew the trick, and she didn't even know there was a trick. He asked if *anyone* knew, and Sally did. She said, "If the number ends in a 0, 2, 4, 6, or 8, then 2 goes into it." Mr. Shoe told Sally she was right, and then asked Lori if 2 went into 796, and Lori said, "I guess so," and he said, "Well, you guessed right." Then he asked the class if everyone knew all the other tricks, not just about 2 but about 3 and 4 and 5 and so on. A few of us did. I kind of did. I figured Theo must have, since in the three days I had been sitting behind him he had solved maybe thirty problems for Mr. Shoe, calling them out, and lots of them had involved dividing by 3s and 4s and 5s and all. But Theo was silent. Mr. Shoe, seeing that few of us knew the tricks, gave them to us. He said, "3 goes into any number whose digits add up to a number divisible by 3; 4 goes into any number whose last two digits are a number divisible by 4; 5 goes into any number that ends in a 0 or a 5"; and so on. He wrote them on the board, asked some of us to try the tricks, said they were very helpful and he had used them often, and then told Todd and Robby to get out in the hall to finish their nonsense.

Soon after this, Theo spoke up. It was the only thing he said that whole class. He said nothing directly to anyone, not even to me, but I heard Theo mutter, up from his gut and into his throat, "I hate him, I hate him, I hate him."

The class ended; the day ended.

I waited for Theo after school. I stood near a corner of the building. Some kids on their way home stared at me and whispered, and I felt like the Stupid New Kid Who Didn't Know Where to Go. I tried to make it clear I was waiting for someone. I stood tall and stretched my neck. I looked back and forth. I checked my watch. I tapped my foot.

Even so, I felt stupid.

More than that I felt alone. I felt that way, sometimes. I was glad to be apart from the other kids, sure, I was *used* to it, really, and they were usually just like Theo had said, boring, stupid, and normal; but sometimes I still felt alone.

I could have rushed home, but I didn't. Rushing home would have been kind of rude, you know, and I didn't want to be rude to Theo. I didn't want him mad at me. I was also curious. Theo had said there was something he needed to show me. Something secret, apparently *very* secret. Like, top secret.

There was a bigger reason, though, why I waited.

You see, my family moved *nine* times before I got to Sherman, nine times before the eighth grade. One town we lived in for all of four months. I don't really remember our house in that town. I mean we barely lived in it, barely got our stuff unpacked, and it was a long time ago besides (when I was really little), but I do remember the night we moved in. None of our furniture was there yet and we sat on the floor as we ate our dinner. We ate fried chicken from a greasy bucket. That night was Halloween night and I didn't get to trick-or-treat. My mom gave me a bag of candy to make up for that. And we were gone from that house before my birthday in March.

I didn't like to move around so much. How could anyone like it? But I had to. My dad changed jobs a lot. And when you move around as much as I did, most of the time you end up stuck with yourself, only yourself, all by yourself. Oh, yeah, I thought about making friends, but never believed in it. Most of my life it had been kind of pointless. Even if I made a friend, which wasn't often, it wasn't long before I'd leave him behind.

But you know what? I never quite gave up.

I had been in this new town for a little over a week. Most places I lived, it'd be months before I even talked to anyone, I mean more than just *Hi* or *What was our home-work assignment last night?* But this town wasn't most places. It had Theo Vee, and Theo Vee had already made *me*, Michael Wilson, his ally. I wasn't sure what that meant, and I know it was kind of scary. Still, by the end of the day I was starting to like the sound of it. *Ally* was almost *friend*.

And that's the biggest reason I stayed after school, waiting for Theo. Maybe he could be a friend. (He'd even said we could be friends if I wanted.) I also felt very bad for him, what with Jeffrey and all. At that point I didn't know who Jeffrey was, exactly—all the stuff I told you about him I found out about later—but I knew very well what it was like to get slugged. And slugged again. I'd even been pushed down some stairs once. But never mind the details. Trust me. I knew what it was like to hate a bully. So even if Theo didn't need my friendship, I figured he could use my sympathy.

Theo soon appeared and came straight at me. He went past, slowing down just enough to snap, "Follow me."

I followed. We marched out of the school yard, looped through the neighborhood, went up and down the main drag, into a hardware store, a corner market, a paperback exchange, pretending to shop, like we were headed to no place special at all. It was obvious that Theo was making sure we weren't being tailed. We didn't talk much. He asked me if I had missed my bus to come with him. I told him I didn't take a bus home from school. "Good," he said. That was about it. When he was sure that no one had tailed us, we marched to where the junkpile was.

Our march there was long. We went off on a back road. A dog followed us, and circled us for a while, but got bored at last and went away. Some cows behind a fence noticed us but didn't moo or anything. In a huge field beside the road we saw a tractor calmly mowing. Soon we came to a long stretch of bushes and trees, like a kind of sudden forest. Theo turned and went in. There wasn't a path but he had clearly gone this way before. No branches swatted or tripped him. I got a little scratched, but I kept up. Oh, yes, I was *utterly* curious by then. Enchanted even. There was no telling what was up, and to be honest I didn't *want* to be told. *Let the dragons at me!* or some such thing. Come what may. Had some Malignant Lord ordered Theo to kidnap me? Who knew!

Suddenly we were out of the forest and on a scraggly patch of grass; and there in a big pile that spilled toward us was the junk.

No, not garbage. No pizza crusts, no moldy beets, no *TV Guide*s from months ago, no Band-Aids used and thrown away, no empty cans of corn. Nope. It was all bits and pieces of furniture, clothing and—more than anything else—appliances, electronics, and machines.

Junk, that is.

Theo muttered, "Don't step on anything, stay there, just a second." So I stayed as he went forward. He stepped carefully, like the pile was eyeing him, too, and might just catch a fright and fly away. He scanned the junk. I asked him what he was trying to find. He said, "Nothing. It'll find me." That made little sense, and I was about to ask for an explanation, I was opening my mouth to ask, when Theo said, "Don't bother me, it'll just be a few minutes, shh."

So I didn't bother him. I just stayed back and waited. What else could I do?

The whole time I waited, Theo was crouching beside the pile, or crawling over it, or digging into it, and finding bits of junk for himself. Actually, he would say, the bits were finding him. After a while he rolled a few handfuls of junk in his shirt, like in a kangaroo's pouch. Then he kept on digging.

It was strange. All the questions I had in my head, about Jeffrey, about the junk, about Theo most of all, and I let myself do nothing for who knows how long, maybe even half an hour, while Theo filled his pouch. I know I told you I wasn't some sort of tranquil lamb, and really I wasn't, but that was only *on the inside* and you've got to keep that straight. On the *outside* I was, let's face it, the babiest of baby sheep. Sometimes I just let myself be led.

Finally Theo said, "Let's go," and he went.

And I, the obedient sheep, followed him home.

My mom had expected me home right after school. I should have called her from school to ask her if I could be late, but I figured I wouldn't be *too* late and so it would- n't matter. As it was, we didn't get back from the junkpile till after dinner, and I knew the first thing I really had to do was go home. But since I was new in town I didn't know my way home, and Theo wasn't about to tell me. I was stuck with him all the way to his house.

I thought his parents would give me directions, but they wouldn't let me go, either. When Theo brought me in they were shocked. He never brought anyone home. His parents just about poked me to see if I was real, and then when I said I *had* to get home, they said no, no, stay for dinner, call your mother, you'll be all right. So I called my mom. I was half hoping she'd yell at me and demand that I come home immediately—I mean, I always want to leave unfamiliar homes; but my mom never was exactly like that and what she actually did was tell me to stay. "Make a friend, Michael," she said to me. Then Theo's mom got on, assured my mom that I'd be no trouble at all, and that's how I ended up eating dinner with Theo and his mom and dad.

Theo didn't really want to eat just then, but his mom almost pleaded with him. Very softly she said, "We held dinner for you," and he gave in with a grumble. As for me, I never have liked eating with strangers, but Theo's mom and dad were nice enough, and, besides, I still didn't know what was up with Theo, the junk, and all of that. If my mom had said I could stay, I would stay.

The dinner was fine. Theo's parents asked about me and my family. At one point they asked where Theo and I had been all afternoon, and I clammed up since Theo had said it was secret; but Theo himself answered indifferently, "Getting junk," and his parents looked at each other almost sadly and didn't ask anything more.

After dinner Theo told me to come down to the basement. He had gone down there earlier to empty his pouch, when I was calling my mom. We went to his father's workroom. Theo turned on the fluorescent lights. There was a table off to the side. On the table were some tools and rolls of wire and, in the middle, the junk from Theo's pouch.

At the table was a stool. Theo brought another one from somewhere in the basement and we sat down. Then Theo said, "Remember, it's a secret. Don't tell anyone. The junkpile's mine. You know about it now, but it's mine. You can't tell anyone. Don't slip up in school, ever. Don't ever talk about it, not even to me, just to be safe. You're my ally. Keep quiet. I hope you never forget how to keep quiet. It's a secret, okay?"

Theo was talking the way he would often talk with me, in a fast bombardment of words. And feeling bombarded, I didn't want to argue with him. I was happy to keep his secret, anyhow.

"Okay," I said.

Theo set to work. He concentrated on his junk. I watched him fiddle for quite a while. I said a few things to him, asked some questions that were kind of lame, but he didn't say much in return. He was making patterns of some kind, laying things out, but who knew what he was working toward.

Finally I decided to ask about that kid with the glassy eyes. Oh, I tried to be very careful. Maybe I shouldn't have brought it up at all, but I was curious, and it was getting too quiet, and I didn't know what else to bring up. So carefully I asked, "Theo, how come that kid slugged you today?"

Theo stopped his work. He gave me a funny, pitying look, like that was the stupidest question so far. Then he frowned. "Why do you think?" His voice was tight.

I shrugged. "He doesn't like you?"

"Ha! He doesn't like anybody."

"But why is he slugging *you*?"

Theo looked at me and frowned some more. "He's slugging me because he's like that. He thinks I'm a sissy." And from there, in a huge bombardment of words, Theo told me about Jeffrey, the colored pencils, and all of that. I asked him about the dead frogs; he told me. And when he was done I said the only thing I could think of to say: "I'm sorry, Theo."

"Sorry for what?"

I shrugged. "For bringing it up."

He frowned again and went back to work. He didn't want to talk after that. Things soon got a bit uncomfortable, but what could I do? I surely couldn't leave. If nothing else, I didn't know my way home.

Luckily Theo's mom came down around nine and asked if I shouldn't be heading home, since it was getting so late. I couldn't believe it was already nine, but it was. I agreed I should go, and she called my mom and gave her directions. I stayed with Theo until my mom got there. He didn't finish whatever he was making before I left, and when I said "See ya later," all he did was grunt.

The next day was a Saturday. I slept in. I liked sleeping in. I didn't get to during the week. Of course I missed all the morning cartoons, but I hadn't watched those since before seventh grade. They bored me. Not enough action. Besides, most of them were for little kids.

I got up, I ate some Froot Loops, I got dressed, I finally turned on the TV and watched the World Wrestling Federation show for a while. It was kind of fake, but it was very cool. My mom was dusting when someone knocked at the door. She answered it and came back and said, "It's for you, Michael."

My first thought was: *Me? but I don't know anyone…*

My second thought was: *Idiot! of course you do.*

Theo was at the door. Don't think I was annoyed because he was there. Of course he had been kind of rude the night before, when he'd been working with his junk and wouldn't really talk to me, and even though I hadn't been offended I had been kind of hurt. But Theo was what

Theo was, kind of rude I mean, and I didn't think he'd meant anything bad by it all. And besides, I knew I had been kind of rude myself, bringing up Jeffrey and all. In a way I was lucky Theo would even come to my house.

I was glad he had come.

"Hi, Theo."

"Hi. Um. My mom remembered what she told your mom about how to get to my house and I just turned it around to come here. I finished what I was making," he showed me a large paper bag, "and I thought you should see it. I wanted to show you. It works. They always do. It's great." He pulled the thing out of its bag. "Took just a 9-volt battery. They always do. I had to add some wires but I've got lots of wires—"

I was starting to feel dumb just standing there with the door half-open, like Theo was some annoying sales-man. I wanted us to just sit down somewhere. I was worried about letting Theo in my house, though. I was afraid my mom would think he was weird. But I didn't want him to go away.

I decided we should sit right there on the porch, on the steps. That would be great. It was fall, but the day was like summer. I knew, however, that unless I said something Theo's bombardment would never let up and we would never sit down. So in between two of his words I blurted out, "Let's sit down, okay?" I waved a hand at the steps. Theo sat without a fuss, and I realized that for the first time I was leading and Theo was following. Just a little bit, but it was a change.

I sat down beside him.

Theo's bombardment continued. "You know, I never know what it's going to be, not until all the pieces have found me. I can sorta tell sometimes. I recognize things, like it looks like I'm getting some audio doojammer or whatever. In this case the speaker was a dead giveaway, but I sorta knew before that anyhow. See? It's a music box."

But it wasn't your normal music box. It looked like a loaf of mechanical bread, and I couldn't tell what was connected to what, or what turned what, or anything. And there were bits of circuitry in there, too, and every music box that I'd ever seen was always just springs and gears. But Theo clipped the battery into the loaf, and sure enough it clanked and whirred and music came out of the speaker, beeping and wooing, but it was music.

"What's that song?" I asked him.

"I dunno. But it does sound familiar, doesn't it?"

It did, but even now I don't know what it was. Just music, familiar music, music that wasn't a stranger at all.

"How did you know how to build this?"

Theo shrugged. "I just knew. The parts find me.

When I've got all the parts there should be, they stop looking for me, and I go home and put them together. They
go together just like they're supposed to. And it always
works. I've got lots of things. I'll show you later. You'll
never guess what any of them do. You have to ask me. But
you can work the switches yourself or put in the batteries.
I've got lots of batteries."

I stared at the music loaf for a while. It almost made
me giggle, since all I could call it was a music loaf, and a
music loaf was a silly thing, but that's what it was, and like
Theo said, it worked.

It was very weird, and I loved it.

I asked him, "How does it work?"

He shrugged. "I dunno. I never do."

"But you put it together."

"I didn't *design* it."

"Wait a second. You picked out the parts—"

"You're not listening to me. I said *they* pick *me*."

He *had* said that, more than once, and I'd heard him
say it. But it just hadn't clicked. It didn't make sense. And
then it really hit me what Theo had been saying. The loaf
had more or less *built itself*. Theo had been *used*...

No. That was nuts.

I shook my head. "Yeah, but how does a bunch of
junk *pick you*? What do you really mean?"

"What do you mean what do I mean? I mean it picks me. Did you forget how to hear? They pick me. Then I put them together. Like I'm supposed to. The way they're supposed to be put together. Get it? I don't decide. I just *know*."

"They tell you?"

"No. I said *I just know.* Get it?"

What was there to get?

Theo got mad. "See! That's what it's like. People always have to know how they work. They don't believe me. They just work, that's all. And they're mine. I made them. The junk picked *me*. I know what the junk wants, that's all. I've got a better brain than everyone else. I know it. I do. The rest of you need things explained. I don't. I can just *do* it. I make things that *work* and I'm so smart I don't even know how they work. I just make them. That's all. Did you forget how to think? Think about it!"

I backed off. Theo was just about hissing and spitting. I couldn't blame him really. It was obvious I'd been incredibly rude. I had been doubting his word, you know, and I was his *ally*, for goodness sake. Some ally I was, doubting him.

Theo calmed down. "I've always been able to do this. It's like the math. I just *know*. It's just there, the answer. I can do any of it. People like *you* need to be told how."

That was snooty. Theo was lumping me with idiots, or so it seemed. I didn't think he was being mean but I didn't much like the insult. And so when he said that people like me needed to be told how, I said, "Yeah, but then I can do it, too."

"Exactly." Theo unclipped the battery and shoved the music loaf back in the bag. "It's like those tricks Mr. Shoe showed us yesterday. I never needed those tricks. Of course 2 goes into 544! Only normal people need tricks to know that. And Mr. Shoe is telling everyone those tricks. Now they can do what I do."

"What's wrong with that?"

Theo made a face. "Nothing, I guess. People can be smarter if they want. But they still won't ever be as smart as me. I'm smarter, that's all. I skipped second grade. I went right from first to third. I'm supposed to be in seventh grade. But I'm too smart for that. I am. I always will be. That's all."

Then he sighed.

So Theo was smarter and knew he was smarter and had skipped a grade because he was smarter. His smarts I already knew about; his skipping ahead, however, was news to me. Of course Theo *had* seemed a little young for eighth grade, maybe kind of immature; but I wasn't so mature myself, I guess, so who was I to say?

After Theo's sigh we sat quietly for a while.

The sun was warm on my arms. From far away I heard the air raid siren. They tested it every Saturday at one o'clock. I'd heard the same kind of thing in my old neighborhood. Actually it was probably just a tornado siren, but calling it an air raid siren was much more exciting. Storms are great for excitement, sure, but bombers are better.

Finally Theo said, "We forgot to plan things yesterday. I said we needed to plan things, to figure things out. We didn't. I forgot. Did you forget? We both did. We still have to plan."

"Plan what?"

"Pratt. I want him wrecked."

And there it was.

"What do you mean?"

"Wrecked. I want to wreck him. I want him wrecked. I don't want him hurt. He should be hurt, a lot, and all the time, but that's not enough. And I don't want him dead either. I do want him dead, but that's not enough. And getting him expelled is stupid. I want every part of him destroyed."

Theo was being scary again, Big-Time Scary. He

meant what he said. He wasn't exaggerating. But I wasn't
shocked. I barely knew Jeffrey but I knew enough to wish
him the very worst. Theo had a right to want what he
wanted, even if, in the end, what he wanted wasn't right.

"But how do we, uh, *wreck* him?"

"You tell me. You're my ally. Aren't you?"

"You mean *this* is why I'm your ally?"

"Well, yeah that's why. You've got to help."

"Theo, I—"

"Are you ratting out on me?"

"No, I'm not, but I thought…"

"Thought what? That we were friends? I told you
we weren't. We're allies. I said that."

I was stung. "I know that! But I didn't know—"

"Will you help me wreck him?"

I looked at Theo. He waited for my answer. He was
frowning, but he didn't seem mad, exactly. He really wanted my help. But wreck another kid? For real? We might
wish it, sure, but Theo meant to *do* it. I felt really squeamish
all of a sudden.

If I said no to Theo, however, that would be it. I
wouldn't be his ally. He probably wouldn't talk to me ever
again. And I didn't want that.

"Why me?" I said at last.

"Why you? Because I don't know you. I never saw

you in grade school. You just got to Sherman. You could-n't know what they say about me. You'd keep my secrets. You're not stupid. You don't look it. I could tell you'd be a good ally. We're mostly the same. I just *knew* it, that's all. *You* picked *me*."

I picked him? That's not how I saw it. But some-thing made bits of junk call out to Theo—maybe that same thing had made me, my person, my body, my soul, who knows, something that was *me* call out to Theo, too, across the school yard early one October morning when he needed an ally most.

And so there I was, Theo's ally.

I couldn't say no to him.

There was a very good reason Theo needed an ally. He didn't know what to do. Wrecking was a new thing for him. It really involved *designing* something, and he was used to things designing themselves. Theo had brains, but his brains did what they did without asking him first. He didn't tell them what to do. Without even thinking he could solve any problem in math or build the oddest things, but when it came to wrecking, Theo was stumped.

Problem was I didn't know what to do either.

Theo snapped, "I know you don't know what to do.

I don't either. Neither of us do. Not yet." He looked back and forth, at the porch, at the front of my house. "Let's get out of here. It's not right for planning. It doesn't feel right. Will your mom let you go? Tell her we're going." He got up. "Tell her."

"Okay, okay."

I asked my mom if I could go out with Theo. She said, "Of course. Did you eat?" I told her I'd had some Froot Loops. "I meant lunch," she said. That *was* my lunch. "Are you sure you won't get hungry?" she asked. "Mom," I whined, "I'm not going to *Mars*." She shook her head and said okay, go.

Good thing she let me go when she did. Theo was already at the corner and not even looking back for me. I had to run to catch up. I asked him why he didn't wait. He asked me why I took so long. "My mom," I said. He grunted.

And then we went to the tunnel.

At the edge of our neighborhood, away from the main part of town, there was a ravine. It was ten or fifteen feet deep. Its sides were almost like slides. One end of the ravine went off to somewhere, on and on and on. You couldn't see where it stopped. The other end stopped right under a neighborhood road; that was where the tunnel began. The tunnel went to the river. In that ravine, rushing into the tunnel, was a creek. Theo and I, like everyone else in that part of the state, called a creek a crick, so that's what I'll call it now, a crick. The crick was about two jumps wide and ankle deep.

Theo and I stood at the edge of the ravine with only a tiny, useless fence of weeds to keep us from falling in. I hoped we weren't going into the ravine, but I knew we were. I hadn't realized, yet, that we were going into the tunnel, too.

Theo said, "Watch out for the rats," and started to slide down. He half-walked, half-fell, feet first, his butt kind of on the ground. His feet pushed some stones and pebbles out of the dirt, which rolled down in front of him and splashed into the crick. He reached the bottom and stood on the very narrow muddy bank. I hadn't even moved.

"Whaddaya mean, rats?" I said.

"Rats," he said. "Did you forget what rats are?"

"No, but I don't want to—"

He frowned. "C'mon. It's not like they're full of diseases. They're just big and black."

"Where are they?"

"Here, there. C'mon already. They never got me."

Oh, wonderful. I followed him down.

"We're going to the river," he said.

"River? What river?"

He pointed into the tunnel. "That river."

I should tell you the tunnel was more like a pipe. It was big enough to let you in, but small enough to make you hunch. Of course it was dark, very dark. From where we were, outside it, you could just see the other end. A circle of light. The river.

I cried, "We're going in *there*?"

"Why not? It's concrete. It won't fall in. I've gone in tons of times before. Never died yet." He grinned. Theo wasn't usually amused. I think my fear was fun for him.

But then he got serious again. "We gotta plan. No one'll hear us in there. The dark'll help us think. C'mon. Grow up." Theo walked to the pipe, stepped onto the rust-stained, pitted concrete, hunched down, and went in. It was all I could do to tell myself: *The pipe didn't eat him. He just went in.*

I had this thing about dark cramped places, you see. I mean, who doesn't? But, bah bah bah, I was a sheep, and in I went behind Theo the Bold.

It actually wasn't *that* dark, not once you were in there. The sun could make its way through little by little.

But it was awkward. I was a hunchback, for sure. And there was a kind of floor, the pipe wasn't perfectly round, but the floor was slanted and messed with a slimy moss that made me slip too many times. My shoes got wet, and my socks. The crick swirled past, cold and making echoes. I touched the wall to hold myself up. The concrete was damp. It chilled my fingertips.

For Theo it was just a walk in the park.

Over his shoulder he said to me, "We'll know when we get out. We'll have our plan. When we get to the river we'll know what to do. Right? When we get out of the pipe, we'll know. So think. Think, think, *think*."

I thought I heard a chittering, like a rat.

"What's our plan?" said Theo. "What do we do?"

It wasn't a rat. I hoped it wasn't. I didn't see a rat. What would a rat look like in there? Just two pinprick eyes, evil, red. That's what it would look like. But I didn't see that. The chittering was just the crick. I hoped.

"So?" said Theo. "What do we do?"

"Uhm—" I slipped, got back on the slant. "Uhm. I dunno. Burn his locker?"

Theo snorted. "No way. What does that have to do with wrecking Pratt? That's stupid. It's simple-headed. It's something Jeffrey Effrey would do." Theo paused. "Scum thinking. Don't think like scum."

We walked and we thought.

You know, it's not easy to force an idea. I thought and I thought and I thought and I thought about Jeffrey—whenever I *wasn't* thinking about staying upright and keeping the rat fangs out of my flesh; but it was all just a jumble.

What to do to Jeffrey?

We were soon far enough in that behind us was just a circle of light. In front of us there was still a circle of light. It didn't seem any bigger. It must have been, but it didn't look it. I wondered, suddenly, if the river would come our way, all fifty bazillion gallons of it. No, it couldn't. The crick went to the river, not from it. Cricks never went backward—did they?

Where were the rats?

The dark wasn't helping *my* thinking.

My shoes started to squish.

Theo said, "We gotta be subtle. You know what *subtle* means? It means we don't burn his locker. We don't do anything obvious and simple and like a delinquent would do. I don't want to ruin Jeffrey's day. I want him wrecked. Go for his mind. Go for his soul. That's the only way. Anything *else*, anyone can do."

"Why don't you make something?"

"Huh?"

"Like a mind and soul wrecker. Make one. You can—" As soon as I said this, I knew where I was wrong.

"I don't *design* things," he cried. "Did you forget?"

I'd forgot.

Never mind then. Back to thinking. After my stupid remark about making things—stupid, because Theo never controlled what he made—I wanted to lighten things up a bit, and half-joking I said, "You know what Mr. Bembo has on his desk?"

"What?"

"It's a little box. He says there's antimatter in it. He says he got a gram of it from an atom smasher in Switzerland. He says the box has a magnetic field that keeps the antimatter from touching any normal matter and totally blowing up. If we go dump the antimatter out of the box onto Jeffrey, Jeffrey'll be destroyed. He'll just go away in a flash of light."

"No, no, no! I don't care about his body. And that's not wrecking him. That's, like, *annihilation*. I don't *want* that. And Bembo's just telling a story anyhow."

"I know that. I was only kidding."

So we walked. We thought. "Think, think," Theo said.

I wasn't that scared anymore. I hadn't been that scared to begin with. Just a little worried. In fact, I was starting to enjoy the creepiness. Then we passed a huge gap in the wall. It was another pipe, connected to the one we were in and going off, who knew where, under the ground. There wasn't any sunlight in this other pipe. It was doom. My heart, my stomach, all of my insides did a somersault—

There were *rats* in there.

I just knew it.

Red and evil pinprick eyes…

Like a ninny I hurried past the gap. I slipped on the moss and knocked my shoulder but didn't fall and didn't slow either. I stopped right behind Theo. He asked me what my problem was. No problem, I said.

Walking, thinking, we talked about some more ideas but came up with nothing good before we reached the river. We scrambled out onto the bank, out of the gloom, without a plan. Theo asked, "Do you have anything yet?" I didn't. He swore and, of all things, kicked the river. He splattered us both.

For a while he fumed. Then he said, "Forget it. Go home. I'll see you later. Bye." He waved like he didn't care, then trudged back into the pipe, heading home. Just like that. I wasn't sure if he expected me to follow. I don't think he did. He seemed to have cut me off for the moment. I wasn't keen on going back in the pipe, anyhow.

"Bye, Theo," I said, shrugging. I was already getting used to his sudden ways. I wasn't offended at all. I didn't even feel abandoned.

It was still like summer out. I took off my soaked shoes and socks and climbed barefoot up the grassy ground around the pipe. I didn't quite know where I was, but the pipe had been straight, and so my house had to be over *there*. So *there* I went, and I only got a little lost.

The next day was a Sunday. Theo didn't come over. I didn't see him. It was a slow day.

I still had some boxes to unpack. The rest of the house was pretty much done. My mom had done a lot in a week, but my room still had boxes in it. I was in no hurry, even though my mom kept nagging me to unpack, but I had nothing else to do so I unpacked for a while.

I didn't feel so good about my talk with Theo. Our planning hadn't seemed that serious the day before, but it was and I knew it. What we were trying to plan wasn't just a simple prank, and it didn't make me feel any better to think we would probably never *really* wreck Jeffrey Pratt.

I didn't change my mind, though. I didn't chicken out. I was still Theo's ally. It was only when I was alone that I got a little squeamish again. Like I said, Theo was scary—the whole thing was kind of scary whenever I stopped to think about it.

But how often could you stop to think around Theo?

Monday, my fifth day at Sherman, was a bad day.

In the morning I was stabbed. Well, maybe not stabbed, but the knife was sharp enough to stab me good and got *this* close to my gut. It happened in the back of Mr. Bembo's room. I was back there looking at the posters on the wall. Mr. Bembo had a chart of the elements that was easily as old as my mom and dad. I was wondering if there were any elements that weren't on the chart—like recently discovered elements—when a kid (who sat two rows over from me) and another kid (who sat behind him) got on either side of me and knocked me with their shoulders. I tightened up. Then the first kid said—more like breathed in my ear—"How much blood you think he's got?" The second kid breathed in my other ear, "Let's find out." And that's when I saw the pocketknife in the first kid's fist. He was scraping the point of it on my shirt.

Looking back on it now, I'm sure those kids never planned to even poke me with the knife. They were just delinquents, that's all. They didn't care about me. They probably didn't even know my name. They just thought they were dangerous men and wanted to make me sweat.

Well, I sweated. I gave them a show. I was scared and I looked it, and I felt foolish for looking scared, and I was sure there was sweat on my forehead, although there probably wasn't. But that's what they wanted, a terrified me.

And as soon as it was clear I was really afraid of them, of getting stabbed, of bleeding all over the floor, of dying in Mr. Bembo's room, the kids laughed like those kind of kids do, nasty and stupid, and left me alone.

I wasn't going to move. I wasn't sure if they were really gone. I didn't leave that chart for a long time. I didn't even turn away from the wall. In fact I missed the bell—I didn't even hear it—and Mr. Bembo had to tell me to sit. Everyone giggled as I went to my seat. It was okay to be scared, I was almost *stabbed*, you know—well, kind of—but I wished I'd had the strength to brush it off more quickly.

A couple of hours later I wasn't any stronger, and that time it was over something far more important.

I was on my way to Ms. Gasperwit's class when I saw Theo at the other end of the hall. He didn't see me. Jeffrey came out of the crowd of kids, right at Theo like a train, and smashed Theo against the wall. Theo hit with a thud, and his books and papers spilled around him. Jeffrey, like he didn't mean to, stepped on Theo's stuff and kicked at it and sent one book across the floor, knocking the feet of some other kid, who almost tripped.

And what did I do? From where I was I couldn't do much, but *all* I did was hide my face. If Jeffrey saw me, he'd attack me, I was sure of that; and if Theo saw me I'd have to help him—I'd have to *try*, at least. He'd hate me if he saw me doing nothing but watching. Maybe he wouldn't hate me; maybe he didn't want anyone's help. That didn't matter. I should have *tried* to help, if only to let him know he was not alone, and not everyone was his enemy. But I was afraid of getting hurt.

Sometimes I was *such* a sheep, you know, from the outside in, completely through and through. I may have been in a bad way to begin with, I mean after that morning's thing with the knife, but that was no excuse. I was being a coward, plain and simple.

I didn't even see how the attack on Theo ended. I ducked into Ms. Gasperwit's room, hating myself all the way.

I saw Theo later in Mr. Shoe's class. I didn't think there was any way I could sit behind Theo—not for a whole class, not for a second—not after the way I had let him down. Luckily he didn't have much to say to me, and he didn't even notice that I wasn't really paying attention. I just nodded and felt awful. Then when class started, Theo turned to the front, and I didn't have to face him again for a while. We both just listened to Mr. Shoe.

You know, Mr. Shoe wasn't very old. He was only twenty-four. But he already had a bald spot and all of us could see it. Some of the kids even teased him about it. Most adults you just don't tease. You know they'll yell at you, or kill you, if you try. But Mr. Shoe was easy to tease.

Near the end of class, when all of us were supposed to be starting our homework, Todd asked Mr. Shoe, "Do you ever play cards?" Mr. Shoe said he did, sometimes. Then Robby asked Mr. Shoe, "Do you ever play balderdash?" Todd and Robby didn't care a bit about any card game called balderdash—Mr. Shoe, however, didn't get it. He thought that Todd and Robby were just chatting with him. He didn't connect *balderdash* with *bald*. He should have. He should have been used to jokes like that. I'd heard enough of them already, and I'd been there only a few days. But Mr. Shoe didn't get it.

And another thing. Some of the kids didn't know how to do the work. They never did. They never listened to Mr. Shoe when he was teaching us. They had to ask him to explain it all again during homework time. And Mr. Shoe always helped them. Once in awhile he'd say to a kid, "Why didn't you listen the first time around?" But you know he was just too wishy-washy to make us listen the first time around, and he never told any of the kids it was their own fault they didn't know what to do.

In a way it was disgusting. Mr. Shoe was so *lame*. He got teased and didn't know it. He let kids ignore him during class and then he helped them with their work. The man seemed completely dim, sometimes, and he had no backbone at all.

I told myself that nobody ever said I had to be brave, and Theo wasn't exactly my friend anyhow. That didn't make me feel any better. Maybe Theo wasn't *exactly* my friend, but he *was* my ally and no one, in any event, had a right to smash him. I felt hurt for him. I got mad at myself. I was ashamed. I knew I had to make up for my cowardice, and so, much as I wanted to go straight home, I met Theo after school. I was supposed to meet him. Early that morning he had told me to meet him. So I met him.

We headed for the junkpile. We took a long and crazy route like before. Theo rubbed his shoulder a few times as we walked. I think he tried to do it casually so that I wouldn't notice. He didn't know I had seen what happened, and he probably didn't want to fill me in.

Jeffrey had me completely mad by then. I may have been kind of mad at myself, but Jeffrey had me furious. He hurt Theo. I hated that. I wondered why Theo wasn't calling Jeffrey every vile name in the book. I didn't ask him why, of course, since then I'd probably have to admit that I'd seen Jeffrey hurt him.

We marched.

Soon Theo asked, "Did you come up with anything yet? Have you been thinking? It's been two days. Did you remember to think about it? What have you got? Well?"

I didn't have anything. I didn't really want to talk about it. But then all of a sudden I was sick of being squeamish. The whole day fell in on me. First the knife, then my hiding, all my anger, fear, and shame—all of it made me feel a *fight* inside. I didn't want to run or be weak. I couldn't let Theo down again. There was wrecking to be done and I, for one, was hot to do it.

Something popped into my head. I asked Theo, "Are you sure you can't make a wrecker?"

"I *told* you—"

"Wait! Listen to me. You don't know why one bit of junk finds you instead of some other bit, right?"

Theo squinted at me. "Uh, right. I don't know. Some find me, some don't. It depends ..."

"Depends on what?"

"On—um, I dunno. On whatever the junk wants."

I shook my head. "Maybe it depends on *you*."

"Huh?"

I was grinning. I had *such* an idea. My feelings had been yanking me around so much that it seemed that feelings could make *anything* happen.

"Your mood!" I cried. "The world treats you differently depending on your mood. If you're grumpy, you get frowns; if you're happy, you get smiles. Right?"

"I guess."

"Well, just be *mad*. Be *mad* right through to your fingers and toes. Make your whole body just one big wish for wrecking Jeffrey and the only junk you'll get'll be wrecker junk."

He scowled. "That's dumb."

"No it's not."

"It won't work."

"It will too."

"No way."

"Yes way!"

Theo opened his mouth, then shut it again. He raised an eyebrow. He shrugged. "Maybe it will work."

"Trust me, it will."

"You might be right."

"I *am* right." I was very pleased with myself.

"We'll see. It could work. It just might. It might, okay? You're *not* stupid. This does help me. I knew you'd help me. I knew it." He nodded. "You *are* a good ally."

I smiled. It was good to hear him say that.

You know I had let Theo down. My idea made up for that. I wasn't a coward anymore, I wasn't stupid anymore, I didn't feel angry anymore, I didn't fear anything anymore. The bad day that had fallen in on me fell right off of me. I was a proper ally now, and we allies had the beginnings of a perfect plan.

Of course we were off to make a wrecker—a weapon, if you like—but you think that made me hesitate? No way. Marching to the junkpile, we were troopers with a mission. *Ahead's the battle!*—we only had to make it happen. The enemy would not escape. Defeat would be his, not ours. *Onward to Glory!*

Yes, indeed, I was anything but a lamb by then. Joy overtook me. I was so joyful I was *fizzy*. Theo seemed as joyful. His face was much less grim. He still moved like a bullet, though, and made sure we weren't being tailed.

As soon as we got to the pile, Theo said, "Don't bother me. Don't talk to me. I gotta concentrate. Okay? You got that? I need to concentrate." Then he added,

"Thanks," and went off to let a wrecker find him.

From Theo that wasn't rude. I didn't mind. In fact, his *Thanks* was downright courteous. Anyhow, I did what Theo wanted. I sat down, crossing my legs, and watched.

Now Theo's face was worse than grim, and both his hands were fists. He squatted down, shifted left and right. Twice, as I watched, his fist shot out, swallowed some junk, and shot back and spat the junk into his pouch. Then he hopped to another spot and squatted again. A couple of times he climbed up on the pile, stretched himself toward the peak, and plucked something with his fingers. Then he climbed down very carefully.

After awhile I laid back and, without exactly meaning to, closed my eyes. I started to daydream, but before I got very far I heard Theo say, "C'mon, get up, I've got everything, let's go." I raised myself and blinked at him. He was standing beside me. His pouch, which wasn't very full, was clamped shut with his hands. Then I noticed the wash of joy on Theo's face. Theo was less frenetic, more simply eager. It was kind of odd.

Theo said, "C'mon. We gotta build this thing."

I stood up, uncrossing my legs. "So you got something?"

"You bet I do."

"Didn't take long."

"Nope."

We traded grins. "Okay," I said, "let's go."

And full of fizz, we rushed to Theo's home.

To get his wrecker, Theo had made himself into a kid-shaped hunk of rage. His fingers, his toes, his knuckles, his knees, his ears, his teeth, his eyes, his heart—every little bit of him just stopped being human for a while. I don't know how Theo got there so completely, but when you think about it he really didn't have that far to go.

I might be exaggerating. It's probably impossible to have raging ears. But Theo did *something* remarkable with himself: he had gone into a kind of trance—or so he said— and as far as I'm concerned that means he did exactly what I had told him to do. He made his body a wrecking wish.

And when he had the junk he needed, he turned it off. Just like that he came out of his trance, and it was such a relief to his body that he became *happy*. It was terrible in a way. He had a weapon, and he was happy.

Terrible or not, that's how it was for him *and* me.

We weren't thinking about Jeffrey anymore. Neither of us felt so very intense, so put upon, so belligerent. We had something unheard of in Theo's pouch: in pieces, yes, but there it was, a genuine Mind & Soul Wrecker; and we,

Theo Vee and Michael Wilson, were going to build it. It wasn't a matter of weaponry anymore, it was simply a matter of science—of magic, if you like.

We couldn't wait. Theo's mom was glad to see me and I was quite polite, thank-you please, and even friendly, but we boys just did *not* have time to eat and so both of us refused dinner. We went straight to the workroom, turned on the lights, poured out the junk, and got to work.

Theo, of course, did the real work. The wrecker's design came to him, not me. *He* arranged the bits of junk. He played with them to see how they fit. I did hand him things when he asked for them. I also cut any wire he needed, using his dad's wire cutters. But mostly I just watched.

I didn't mind being off to the side. It didn't mean I was unimportant. I knew that. Theo was simply doing what only he could do. Watching him suited me just fine. I was too fizzy to gripe, and there was no reason to gripe anyhow.

Sometimes Theo worked very fast, sometimes very slow. But at one point it had been so long since he'd done anything that I had to ask him, "Is it done?" I could tell it wasn't *done* done, I mean like ready to use. Theo hadn't connected anything yet. All I meant was: *Is it time to put it together?*

Theo knew what I meant. "No."

No problem. I was ready to watch some more.

"No," he said, "it's not done. A piece is missing."

"Really?" I scanned Theo's lap, my lap, the floor around our stools, under the table, all the way to the door. I didn't see so much as a screw. "You think we dropped it on the way home?"

"No, you don't get it. I didn't *lose* a piece. I never had it. It didn't pick me when I was there. It's missing."

"You mean it wasn't in the pile at all?"

"Maybe. No, no. I just went too fast. I was so excited, I went too fast. I didn't wait for things to be right. I thought they were right before they were. I left a piece behind."

"So should we go back and get it now?"

Theo sighed and looked at the ceiling. "No, I don't feel like it. It's a long walk. It's okay. We'll do it tomorrow."

That wasn't like Theo. I had expected him to jump off his stool and rocket to the junkpile. "You okay, Theo?"

He smiled at me. "Yeah, just kind of whipped. Forget it. We can finish tomorrow."

You know what? I think Theo was feeling so all-around good about things, despite the missing piece, that he could be patient for once. Imagine that.

■   ■   ■

We didn't have anything to do, exactly, but I didn't want to leave. Theo didn't ask me to. He didn't even act like he wanted me to, but I really didn't want to leave, so I said, "Can I see your other things?"

"What?"

"Your other things. You said I could see them."

He thought back for a moment. "Yeah, right, I did say that." He jumped off his stool. "C'mon, they're this way. You'll never guess what they do. Grab that sack of batteries." He went out of our bright patch of fluorescent light, past his father's workbench, toward a closed door. There was a sign on the door—one of those black and yellow RADIOACTIVE FALLOUT SHELTER signs. Written on the sign in black marker was *Theo's Things.* Theo opened the door, reached around to flick on the light, and then went in. As soon as I'd found the sack of batteries, I grabbed it and followed Theo.

The walls in the room had metal shelves. Some shelves were empty; on all the rest were Theo's Things. They were *things*, all right, tightly built handfuls and armfuls of junk. And every one of them had a battery clip and a switch.

Theo said, "Be careful. Don't touch them. Ask me first. Gimme a battery." He had his hand outstretched and was wiggling his fingers. I gave him a battery. "Now untie your shoe," he said. I gave him a funny look. "Just do it, okay?" I did it.

He carefully took a balled-up Thing from a shelf and clipped in the battery. He set the Thing on the ground. "This one's great," he said. He was crouching behind it. He turned its switch on, and with a pop its legs came out from around its body. The legs were bits of pipes and tubes with little wheels for joints and what looked like kite strings for muscles. The Thing was a spider.

It shuddered for a moment, not sure what to do, and then it shot for my untied shoe, chattering, clattering—a tinny, awful, rapid-fire tinkling of scrambling metal spider legs. I yelped and stumbled back but Theo yelled, "Stay put!" So I swallowed my gut and let the spider at my shoe. It covered my shoe. Its legs tinkered and tugged, and I was watching for blood but none came, and then the spider clattered backward and was still.

My shoe was tied.

Theo said, "It's a spider that ties your shoes."

I stared at it and thought, *You must be kidding.*

"Wait, wait," Theo said, scurrying from shelf to shelf. "Wait, check this out, gimme a battery, quick." I got a battery out of the sack, not quick but slow, afraid I'd startle the spider, and tossed it to Theo. He caught it and clipped it in another Thing: a tricycle wheel with junk in its rim and a speaker at the hub.

Theo said, "Okay now. As soon as I roll it, just say *Wheel!* to get the wheel's attention, and then say a word."

"Huh?"

"Say *Wheel!* and then a word."

"Uh, wha, okay." I was keeping an eye on that spider.

Theo gave the wheel a push. It was rolling itself after a moment. The tire turned; the junk inside stayed level. It must have had a motor inside. It was going around the room. It was like it knew where the walls were. It tilted itself to turn but never fell over.

"Get its attention," Theo snapped.

"Uhm—Wheel!" If that got the wheel's attention, it sure didn't let on. It rolled around all the same. And then, having no idea what to say, I cried, "Dog!"

The wheel replied, "Cat."

That was weird.

"Say something else," Theo told me.

"Uhm…I dunno. Fat."

"Get its attention first!"

"All right, okay." I watched the wheel roll and roll. "Wheel!" I yelled. "Fat!"

The wheel replied, "Thin."

I stared at Theo. I know my mouth hung completely open. He grinned, nodded, and said, "Say something else."

"Uh—Wheel! Big!"

The wheel replied, "Small."

Theo said, "It's a wheel that contradicts you."

"You *can't* be serious."

"You saw for yourself!"

"But it's—it's—"

"It's *what*?"

I threw up my hands. "Amazing."

"Of course it is."

I watched the wheel. A thought occurred to me. "What if I said something like, I dunno, *eraser*?"

He shrugged. "If a word doesn't have any kind of opposite, the wheel just gets confused. Try it. See what it says."

"Wheel! Eraser!"

The wheel replied, "Gastroenteritis."

Theo said, "See what I mean?"

The wheel, rolling along, avoided the spider. The spider didn't seem to notice—it just stood there, silent, still, and sucking on its battery.

"Okay, c'mere," Theo said, waving me closer. I stepped around the spider, let the wheel go by, and put myself next to Theo. "Gimme a battery." I did. "Now put out your hands, like flat, together, palms up." I put the sack of batteries down at my feet and put out my hands like Theo said. He took a cubical Thing off a shelf, clipped in the battery, set the Thing on my hands, and turned it on. I felt tiny puffs of air on my palms, and the Thing started bouncing up and down, up and down, on the puffs of air, and after awhile I realized it was bouncing in a certain way.

Theo said, "It's a box that dances."

I watched the dancing box. The puffs of air were tickling me. I almost giggled. I couldn't believe it. I loved it.

Theo grabbed the sack and went to another shelf. Behind me stood the spider, the wheel went around me, the box danced on in my hands. Theo clipped a battery into another Thing and turned it on and let it loose and it flew away. It was a bird.

"Wow," I said, "that really flies."

"Yeah, but that's not what it *does*. Wait."

We watched it flap and flap above our heads; a few times it swooped around us, then went back up high. After a minute or so Theo grabbed at the bird, caught it, and turned it off. With his thumb and finger he pinched something glassy out of its belly. He held it up so I could see. It was a tiny bottle and it was maybe a third full of what looked like water.

"Is that water?" I asked.

"Yep. It's a bird that makes water."

"Out of the air?"

"Uh-huh. Whenever you're thirsty."

"How do you keep it from flying away?"

"It flies in circles. It stays around you."

"And it makes water out of the air."

"That's right."

"Can I drink it?"

"Sure." He handed me the bottle. The water was a squirt of ice. It was wonderful. It made me realize how thirsty I had been.

Theo showed me more of his Things. He told me what kinds of junk they were made of. He let me turn some of them on. I chose some myself to try, and he let me try them. All of them were as odd as the box, the bird, the spider, and the wheel—and every one of them left me in flabbergasted delight.

After a while Theo called it quits. He was tired of showing off, and, besides, his mom brought down some food, dinner warmed over, and by then we were hungry enough to accept it. We caught all the Things that were running, turned them off, and unclipped their batteries.

The batteries we put back in the sack. Then we each cleared a spot on Theo's worktable, away from the unfinished wrecker, and we ate.

Eating, of course, is a great time to think. It's usually a bother to talk with food in your mouth, even when you can do it, and your mom tells you not to do it, anyhow. When you're chewing, it's easier just to think. So I thought.

The first thing I thought of was that my mom didn't know where I was. I hadn't called home. I just about choked on my food. I told Theo I had to go call home. He mumbled okay and I went up to the kitchen. Theo's dad was in there getting a pop and he said hi. I said hi, and asked if I could use the phone, and he said sure. I called and just like before, my mom wasn't mad. She said she had figured I was with Theo. She told me not to be too late but if I was, if it was dark before I left, she could come get me. I told her I didn't need a ride; I could walk home myself. She asked if I knew the way. I kind of did. I knew enough by then. "All right, sweetheart," she said, and we said good-bye.

I never really liked it when she called me sweetheart, but what can you do? Moms can get so *affectionate* sometimes.

By the time I got back downstairs, Theo was done

eating. He was messing around with some tools and stuff, organizing them or rummaging through them, or something like that. He said, "Go ahead, finish eating," and so I did.

While I chewed, I thought.

Now, I was no scientific genius, I didn't know much science at all, but I'd been around long enough, you know, and it seemed to me that Theo's Things weren't playing by the rules—by the laws of nature, that is. I mean, how could they do so much, and do it for so long, running on measly nine-volt batteries? You'd think they'd need tiny nuclear reactors inside. And that bird? Theo told me it was mostly just refrigerator parts. How could something like that fly around and turn air into water? How could a tricycle wheel with some stereo circuits inside know enough to steer itself and contradict you?

Oh, I didn't want to doubt even one of Theo's Things. They were just too cool for bad feelings like doubt. I *believed* in them; I mean, I *had* to. They were *real.* I'm not making them up and I wasn't, like, hallucinating. They really worked. But, man, they didn't make sense. All I could figure was that if you put certain bits of junk together in a certain way, the way Theo did, you'd get a Thing that simply *had* to work. You couldn't help it. Like, if you put a ball at the top of a pointy hill and let go, the ball has to roll down. That's how it is. Theo's Things probably weren't breaking any rules—they were just following the rules in the only way they could.

Maybe, maybe not.

The spookiest part was that Theo didn't design his Things. He said he just *knew* the designs. That could mean the designs were *given* to him. I once thought the music loaf had used Theo to build itself. Maybe the loaf and all his Things had been the ghosts of strange machines, until one day they whispered in Theo's head and got him to make them real.

I finished eating, put my knife and fork in the middle of my plate, and went over to Theo's side. He was still messing with the tools. I watched him for a while. He was in a very decent mood. I figured I could get away with some stupid questions.

"You know, Theo, your Things are really cool."

"I know."

"Are they really made of junk?"

"Looks that way."

"Is all the junk from the pile?"

"Yeah. I do get some stuff from Radio Shack."

"Like what?"

"Stupid stuff. Wire, switches, battery clips, batteries. The nuts and bolts and stuff like that I get from my dad."

"But the rest is from the pile?"

"Yep, all of it."

"And you really don't design your Things?"

"That's what I said."

"Then who does?"

"Nobody."

"Nobody?"

"Right."

"But how—"

"Nobody designs them. The designs are just there. I know them, that's all. I'm smart enough to *see* them. The junk knows I'm smart and picks *me* to put everything together. That's all." Theo was holding a hammer; he let it go. It fell in a box with some other tools. He went over to his table and sat down.

I didn't know what to say next. I was starting to lose my way. I was getting confused again. I went and sat on my stool. I faced Theo. He wasn't getting grim or anything. He was still calm.

"Theo, did—how—um. How long have you been going to the pile?"

"You gonna ask me questions all night?"

Uh oh. "I'm just curious. We *are* allies, you know."

That got him. "So I should answer your questions?"

"Well, yeah. Will you?"

"I guess so."

"Good. Um. So?"

"So what?"

"So how long you been going there?"

"Since August."

"Do you go every day?"

"Mostly."

"Was the junk already there?"

"Some of it."

"The pile was smaller?"

"It almost wasn't there."

"Where's the junk come from?"

"It's just tossed there, I guess."

"By who?"

"I dunno."

"Um. How did you *find* the junkpile?"

I should have known what Theo would say. He said, "I didn't find it. It found me."

Of course. "But how?"

"I was out walking far from everything, and..." He left it hanging there. I finished for him: "And it found you?"

"Yep."

"Um." What next? What could I ask? I didn't think Theo was hiding anything. He was telling me all that he knew, all that he wanted to know. *He* wasn't frustrated by the mystery. I was.

I dropped it. I didn't want my stupid frustration to ruin the day. There was no reason to get bent out of shape. Let it *go*, I told myself.

"Okay," I said, like I was satisfied.

"Anything else?" Theo asked.

"No, that's all."

"Okay. Whatever." He looked me square in the face. "Let me ask *you* something. You really like my Things?"

I didn't have to pretend I did. Quite honestly—quite fizzily—I told him, "Yeah, Theo, I do, a lot."

"Good. You should. They're great. But they're a secret. Keep them a secret. Don't forget we're allies."

"I won't, Theo. I won't."

So I told Theo I wouldn't forget we were allies. I meant it, too. And after that it seemed to me there was nothing more to say or do that day. It was getting late and the sun would be setting. It was time to go. Theo agreed. We picked up our dishes and left the basement.

The wrecker was still down there, of course, in the dark, missing a piece, unbuilt but arranged on Theo's table.

The next day, my sixth day at Sherman, was

All–Together Day—a day, the teachers told us, for all us kids to come together. The day was Ms. Gasperwit's idea, and the principal had liked it. He said it was in line with the mission statement of the school, which said, in part, that Sherman would "endeavor to bring all of our students to a state of caring for others." The principal said that Tuesday, October 11, would be All–Together Day for the eighth-graders. The seventh-graders would have the 18th, and the sixth-graders would have the 25th. Most of the teachers went along with this only because they knew Ms. Gasperwit would sulk if they didn't. We kids went along with it only because we had to.

So we met in Ms. Gasperwit's room in groups of fifty, during first, second, and third hours. Her room was de-signed for small assemblies and even had its own stage with lighting and simple rigging. The room and its stage suited Ms. Gasperwit, who just *lived* for the theater. Her walls were plastered with pictures of playwrights and reproductions of folio pages and old posters from Broadway musicals. There were photos, too, of plays she had been in, like *Hamlet*, *Our Town*, and *Guys and Dolls*.

Our groups were alphabetical and Ms. Gasperwit hated that. She said alphabetizing people was *oppressive*. But the principal said it was most efficient, so that's how it was, and that's why Theo and I were in the same group. I was glad. I figured we'd sit together. I wasn't thinking we'd talk about wrecking and all, although we did do that a little. I just thought that allies like us could, well, you know, be *pals* once in awhile—I mean, why couldn't we be?

When I got to the room, Theo was already sitting in the last row, in the corner seat. I sat next to him before any strangers could. I wasn't sure he was glad to see me, but he did nod and say hi to me.

"Now boys and girls"—Ms. Gasperwit always called us boys and girls, like we were in nursery school—"this earthly world of ours can be a trial sometimes, and I know it. We all know it. We feel it in our hearts. And sometimes our hearts are hurting. We feel so alone. Doesn't aloneness hurt? It hurts me—"

Theo and I, back in the last row, were pretty well hidden from Ms. Gasperwit. We could talk if we wanted to. Normally I never spoke up in class, not if I could help it, and Theo spoke up only to call out his answers in math. But Ms. Gasperwit was already boring me to total death, and Theo, I think, felt the same.

Theo said, "You've got her, don't you?"

"Yeah, for English."

"Does she always talk like that?"

"Like what?"

"Like she's all *gooey* inside."

"Yeah, I guess so."

"How dumb."

We chuckled—but quietly, so she couldn't hear us.

"Boys and girls," said Ms. Gasperwit, "our aloneness comes from not being accepted as we are. People don't accept us, we don't accept ourselves. All of us are special. But you're not alone in your specialness—"

Theo said to me, "Don't forget where we're going later." He meant the junkpile.

"Don't worry, I won't."

"We'll finish it tonight." He meant the wrecker.

"Okay." I paused. "You know, I was thinking…"

"Thinking what?"

"Shouldn't we test it first?"

"Why?"

"Just to make sure."

"Maybe. Test it on who?"

"I dunno."

Ms. Gasperwit said, "It's true! Your specialness is shared with other children *just like you.* Let me show you. Erica, Patty, Robin, Matthew, come up here on the stage with me."

That got our attention—and everyone else's. When a teacher starts calling out names, you'd better listen up. *Your* name might be next. Hide yourself well…

Erica, Patty, Robin, and Matthew didn't go up on stage too quickly. I didn't blame them. Who wants to go up on a stage? But still they went, dragging their feet, looking down.

Ms. Gasperwit herded them to a spot on the stage. "This is our first Self-Esteem Zone," she said. "Wonderful! Now Nathan, Gretchen, Alex, and Justin. Come join us!"

Those four went up indifferently, like the first four, and were given their own spot, too, their own Self-Esteem Zone.

"Now, Donald, Cheryl, Heather, and Monica!"

Those four went to their Zone. The rest of us were tensing up, just waiting to be completely embarrassed.

"Now Eddie, Craig, Louise, and Becky!"

Those were the last four, thank goodness. As soon as they were put in their Zone, Ms. Gasperwit declared, "That's all. So all of you," she said to the sixteen kids on the stage, "can you feel your specialness? Do you see how there really are people just like you? And you don't have to feel alone?"

Theo said, "How about Monica?"

"You'd test it on *her*?"

"Why not? She lies all the time. She says she's from Paris and I know she's from Kansas."

"Well, I guess she'd be okay—"

"How about Eddie?"

"Maybe."

I stared at Eddie for a moment. Then it hit me. He had glasses, and the other kids in his Zone—Craig, Louise, and Becky—had glasses, too. I looked at the kids in the Zone next to Eddie's. None of them had glasses. But all of them—Donald, Cheryl, Heather, and Monica—were *tall*. The kids in the next Zone—Nathan, Gretchen, Alex, and Justin—didn't have glasses and weren't tall, but were very *big*. The kids in the first Zone—Erica, Patty, Robin, and Matthew—didn't have glasses, weren't tall, weren't very big… I didn't know *what* they had in common, not at first. Then Matthew opened his mouth. Braces. And I remembered Erica had braces. And I'd seen Patty with a retainer. And yes! Robin had braces, too.

Ms. Gasperwit went to each Zone and spread her arms to hug the space around the kids. She said some happy things.

Theo said, "Eddie eats insects, you know. I've seen him chomp grasshoppers in half."

Yuck. "No he doesn't."

"Yes he does! Pretty sick, huh?"

"Completely. What about Louise?"

"Test it on her?"

"Why not? She thinks she's Miss High and Mighty."

"You're right, she does. But Donald is just as bad. He thinks anyone who can't catch a football is just lowlife scum. And he tackles you in *touch* football."

"Yeah, I heard."

Done with her hugging, Ms. Gasperwit cried, "Children! All of you, each of you! Even though you have something that makes you different—glasses, braces, height, or weight—it also makes you the same! Just like someone else! And you must esteem yourselves! Everyone, esteem them with me!"

Theo said, "What's she talking about?"

"I dunno."

"Hey." Theo grinned. "Why not test it on her?"

"You mean on *her*? Ms. Gasperwit?"

"That's what I said. You forget how to hear?"

I winced. Then I tried a smile. "Naw, it'd be a waste. She doesn't have a mind to wreck."

We chuckled good over that one.

That got us talking about the teachers we had and what they were like. I found out that Theo had Mr. Fusillade, too, just like me, although for a different hour. Right away we agreed he was kind of weird, and as Ms. Gasperwit carried on we talked—we whispered of course—about weird old Mr. Fusillade.

Let me tell you, Mr. Fusillade was something else.

He was always sniffling, scrunching up his nose, making a nostril wide. Every so often he'd pick a speck out of his eye. You weren't even sure there was a speck, but Mr. Fusillade'd pick it out. They said that Mr. Fusillade's arms were full of tattoos: skulls, hearts, knives, girls, snakes, hawks, and words in banners. Dog tags hung from his neck. That's what they said. Sure, no one ever saw the tattoos or the tags, but they were there. Mr. Fusillade's hair, black but streaked with gray, was short now, but they said that long ago it had been pulled back tight in a ponytail.

Theo said that Mr. Fusillade had been a mercenary.

I didn't believe him. Heck, I didn't believe most of what they said about Mr. Fusillade. But Theo swore it was true, and I had to admit that Mr. Fusillade looked like he might have been a mercenary. Of course I'd never seen a *real* mercenary before. I wondered if one of his tattoos said *Death to the Enemy Hordes*.

It was Mr. Fusillade who had started all this stuff about tattoos and all. I'm sure he was only teasing us. Once the rumors about him had got around, he'd smirk from ear to ear and deny them all. So who knows, really.

Sometimes Mr. Fusillade teased us by being, well, kind of morbid. I mean, once he went on about his poor, poor, pitiful body. He had been young once, you know, and it showed. He was one of those people who didn't grow old so much as they wore out. His youth was sagging on him. And once upon a time, he told us, he had been wounded a lot. He called himself *perforated*. He said that all the holes and gashes in him, although they were closed up now, would still gang up on him someday soon and make one *humongous* gashing hole out of his worn-out self.

See? He could get kind of morbid. But he said it all with his giant smirk, and we had to laugh.

So Theo and I talked about old and morbid Mr. Fusillade—and you know what happened after that? The both of us, Theo and I, fell into this gross kind of conversation. I could say I got sucked into it, but that would be a lie. I mean, it was fun. I *liked* it. We told each other stories about wounds, assaults, and accidents, some of them real and some from books, stories about pain and pus, flattened fingers, sizzled skin, chopped-up arms, bloody puddles, stitches, catgut, sewn-up kids, chewed-off toes, greenish stumps, melted eyeballs, blistered palms, shattered knees, and on and on.

Meanwhile Ms. Gasperwit directed some role plays with kids. When the kids were done with their roles, they went back to their Zones. Now they were all back, the plays were done, and Ms. Gasperwit said to all of us, "We're all so different but that must be respected. Our different-ness is a plus. What we are makes us what we are. Come together, now, come together," and she herded the sixteen kids out of their separate Zones and into a single group. "Now, all together, we have one big Self-Esteem Zone! We're all just people, all of us!"

"This is really stupid," Theo said.

"Yeah. I'm glad I'm not up there."

"Me, too." Then suddenly Theo frowned. It wasn't because of Ms. Gasperwit or the gross stuff and all. He had just thought of something. He said, "No. We don't need to test it."

Huh? Oh. The wrecker. "You sure?"

"Sure I'm sure. I made it, didn't I? It'll work. All my Things always work. It'll do what it's supposed to do. It'll work, I know it will. It has to. It can't do anything else."

I couldn't argue with that. I certainly didn't *want* to argue with that. If Theo said the wrecker would work, it would work. No need to test it on anyone. Jeffrey would get it first and get it for sure.

I said to Theo, "Okay."

We didn't whisper about anything more. Ms. Gasperwit kept on for a while about coming together in our differentness, and then she wrapped it up, let the kids go from the stage, and finally dismissed us all to our normal classes.

And that was it for All–Together Day.

■   ■   ■

Ms. Gasperwit didn't make a whole lot of sense. I mean, if we're all supposed to come together, it seems really stupid to talk on and on about how different we all are. And then when she jumped from that to say we're all just people, really, like we're not so different after all—well, maybe we are and maybe we aren't, but that wasn't enough to bring *me* together with the likes of, say, a Jeffrey Pratt.

But I didn't think about it all too much. Ms. Gasperwit was always saying muddy things like that, and I always tried to ignore her. Life was simpler that way.

On the way to the junkpile that afternoon, after we hadn't said too much at all, I asked Theo if he had any comic books, like me. He told me he had a lot. So we talked about what we had: *The Meganauts*, *The Psychic Avengers*, *True War Tales*, *Scorpion Man*, *Sgt. Fist*. Turns out we had a lot of the same. We both had the *Q–Men*, too, but Theo didn't have *Q–Men* #108, like me. That was a valuable issue. By then it was worth over ten dollars, although I'd bought it new for only seventy-five cents. It was worth more than money, though. I would never have sold it. I mean, that's the one where the Razor Kid is atomized by Doctor Null, rebuilt by a nuclear data beam, and turned into the Dark Edge, a zombie godman who splits planets, eats suns, swats away fleets of starships, and starts a Galactic War against the Q–Men, who used to be the Razor Kid's friends. That issue was just too great to ever sell.

I told Theo he could read my #108. He nodded.

A little later on in our march I asked Theo if he had any idea what the wrecker's missing piece would look like. Of course he didn't know. He wouldn't know until it picked him.

"But don't you kind of know already?" I asked. "You do know where it's supposed to go, don't you?"

He frowned and said, "Yeah, I guess. Oh, I dunno. It'll be, like… no. It doesn't matter. I shouldn't try to know."

I shrugged. "Have you ever had missing pieces before?"

"No."

I thought about that. Now I frowned. "Maybe it's because of what we're doing."

"Huh?"

"We're kind of forcing a certain kind of Thing. You never forced it before. What you got was what you got. Now we're trying to get a wrecker and nothing else."

Theo raised an eyebrow. "Yeah, we are forcing it."

"Maybe that's making things mess up."

He shook his head. "Nothing's messed up. We're just missing a piece. I went too fast, that's all. I was too excit- ed. Don't rat out on me."

"I'm not, I'm not! I was just thinking…"

"Well, don't."

"Okay." I shut up.

I think Theo was more worried than he let on. A missing piece was unusual. He was a little bit grim again. I sighed and thought about other things: comics, drawings, homework, TV, potato chips, even Halloween. I wondered if Theo and I would still be allies by the end of the month. Once Jeffrey was wrecked, would that be it? Probably. Mission accomplished—end of alliance. Well, maybe afterward we could be like pals, like we'd been in Ms. Gasperwit's room.

But no, probably not, the way Theo was. And that made me sad.

With my mind on other things I wasn't watching where I was walking, and at the end of a gravel driveway I tripped on a rock and fell. I skinned my palms, not terribly, but enough for spots of blood. Theo stopped and asked me if I was okay. I told him I was. He waited for me to hurry up, made sure I was walking, and then went on. I followed, marching onward, pressing my palms together to press away the sting.

We reached the junkpile.

Theo, grim as ever, left me and walked around the pile. He glared at one piece of junk, then another; neither picked him. He walked around some more. Then he stood like a pole, his arms crossed, and waited.

I waited, too. I stood back a ways, watching. I pressed one of my palms with my fingers. I was tempted to lick it, to clean it out, but I didn't want to get my tongue all gross.

We waited.

Theo hadn't found the missing piece. He was still standing solid in his wrecking rage. I pictured his body, intensely mad, just ripping his muscles and crushing his bones and then hurling him apart. But Theo stayed thoroughly solid, like some kind of infuriated gargoyle.

It was taking a long time. I began to wonder if Theo would ever find that missing piece. And then I thought that maybe he never would. Maybe he wasn't supposed to find it. If he found it, we'd have our wrecker. We'd be able to wreck Jeffrey. And maybe that was wrong. Wrecking him, I mean. Jeffrey deserved it, yeah, but still—oh, I was just being weak again...

All of a sudden Theo snapped out of his gargoyle thing and hurled himself into the pile. He went in so fast he must've knocked his head and scratched his arms, but in he went, digging deep, like some kind of mad mole. And out he came with the piece in his fist.

I couldn't tell what it was. Metal, twisted, flat, marks of paint. Theo held it up and turned it, like he was catching light in a jewel. "This is it," he said, mostly to himself. "It was there all the time. It was there yesterday. I just couldn't hear it. It couldn't pick me. It was buried too deep. But I've got it now. I've got it now. I've got it. Got it. Yes, yes, yes!" Theo clapped the piece in both his hands. He pressed it tight against his gut and, all bright and wild, he took off.

"Hey, Theo!" But he didn't hear me or didn't listen. I took off after him, into the forest, twigs slapping at my face.

Theo got away from me. When I got out of the forest, he was *gone*. I didn't know anyone could run that fast. I bet he cut through the fields and yards on his way home. I stayed on the roads and streets and didn't see him anywhere. I pretty much kept running, though, even with him out of sight.

I found his house. I was out of breath. I really should've walked some of the way. I got my breath back slowly. Then I knocked on his door. His mom answered. "Why, Michael," she said, "come in. How are you?" I told her I was fine. I asked her if Theo had come home. "Well, yes, he ran in a short while ago. I thought he was being chased. He wasn't, was he?" She sounded worried. "Only by me," I said. I kind of smiled. She was relieved. "That's good. Well, he's in the basement. As always."

"Thanks," I said. "Can I go down there?"

"Of course."

So down I went. Theo was already building the wrecker. He hadn't connected anything, but he was fitting things together. When he noticed me he said, "Where have you been?"

Where do you think? "Chasing you."

"You should run faster." He actually meant that as advice. He wasn't being snotty. Okay, Theo. Next time I'll run faster. I nodded and sat on my stool.

So in a basement, like underground, in a harsh fluorescent light, we built our wrecker. It wasn't mechanical. There was nothing to whir or click or ping or hum. Nothing moved. It was only wire, scraps of metal, and electrical parts. Theo pointed out the parts to me and told me their names: resistor, capacitor, fuse, rheostat, integrated circuit. "I don't know what they all do," he said, "I just know their names."

Theo put the parts together using this stuff called *solder*. Solder is soft and silver and easily bent and comes on a spool like a thick thread. You unwind a little, touch the end to the two parts you want to connect, and then, using a soldering iron, which has like a hot pencil tip, you melt the solder and kind of glue everything together.

When you melt the solder, it makes this curly gray and ugly smelling smoke. Now I hear that you're supposed to wear goggles when you're soldering. Theo and I weren't wearing goggles. The smoke stung our eyes. And it really did have an ugly smell. You know what rotten eggs smell like? Well, solder smoke doesn't smell exactly like rotten eggs, but it's that same kind of evil awfulness. I don't know what you'd call it, really, except ugly. It did make me think of demon fires, like that hellfire and brimstone you hear about.

Anyhow, we built the wrecker. Theo did the real work, of course. I just handed him what he needed. There were lots of parts and lots of soldering. But then the wrecker was done. It wasn't very big. It was about the size of, well, a golf ball—bigger than that, though, when the battery was clipped in.

"So what's it do?" I asked him.

"It's a wrecker. It wrecks."

"No, I mean *exactly*. Don't you know?"

"Of course I know. I always know. When I'm done building a Thing I always know what it does. Sometimes I even know before I'm done." He held up the wrecker on the tips of his fingers. "This Thing will wreck Jeffrey. It'll shatter his mind. It'll burst his soul."

Theo was being very poetic. But I guess poetry sometimes comes with genius and only fancy words'll do.

I stared at the wrecker. It really was small. I had kind of expected it to be big, like an atom bomb. Of course even an atom bomb isn't *that* big, compared to what it does. Still, the wrecker was small, and even though it was complicated there was something *crude* about it. It was just a kind of bomb, you know, like a grenade. Was that the best our alliance could do? There was nothing subtle about it, really. *Kaboom!*—and that was it.

Where was our clever plan?

I said to Theo, "Now what?"

He seemed unsure. "We use it."

"How?"

He frowned. "One of us takes it, goes up to Jeffrey, and turns it on."

"But—" I stared at the wrecker. I pictured all the power swirling inside it, the fires of demons hissing out through the cracks, wild to cover and choke and destroy. "But I don't wanna be around when it goes off. It might wreck me, too."

Theo raised an eyebrow. "You might be right. The wrecking could be spread out over two people. That might make it weaker. Jeffrey won't get totally wrecked."

"Yeah! And I might get *partly* wrecked!"

"That too. Well, just don't hang around. Turn it on, toss it, and run away."

"Run away."

"Yeah. Just run away."

How noble. "Which one of us?"

"We'll take turns."

This is what we decided to do. Theo would first try to catch Jeffrey on the way to school. If that failed, he'd try again during second hour, during Mrs. Stencil's art class. If Theo was lucky, sooner or later Jeffrey might be by himself, maybe back by a kiln or something, and Theo could ambush him then and wreck him. Theo would make sure the moment was right, however. He didn't want to rush it all and maybe stumble and so give Jeffrey a chance to escape or, even worse, a chance to smash Theo and crush the wrecker. "I'll take it slow," Theo said, and to be honest a slow Theo would've been quite a sight, but I believed he would be careful.

If Theo's mission failed, I'd get my chance. Sherman, you see, had three lunch periods. Theo had first lunch; I had third. Guess who also had third. That's right. Jeffrey. Before I went to lunch, Theo would get me the wrecker. I probably couldn't ambush Jeffrey in the lunchroom, not with all those kids and monitors around, but I was supposed to try.

And if *my* mission failed, we'd try after school.

Oh, and any time I had the wrecker and I happened to cross Jeffrey's path, in the hall or wherever, I'd try to wreck him. The same went for Theo, any time *he* had the wrecker.

You might wonder why we didn't do something clever, like put the wrecker in Jeffrey's locker. Picture it. Jeffrey opens his locker, the wrecker comes on, and *fwoomp!* one less bully. But to do that, of course, we'd need to break into his locker. In fact, any kind of trick like that would've taken a lot of fuss, and we might have even accidentally wrecked somebody else. At least if we simply tossed the wrecker, only Jeffrey would get it. And besides, Theo was too eager to be clever. He wanted Jeffrey wrecked as soon as possible. Tossing was the quickest way.

So that was our plan. I wasn't real gung-ho about it. I didn't want to risk catching even a bit of the wrecker's power. And now that we had the wrecker and Jeffrey was, like, in our crosshairs, I felt kind of *oogy*. Calm, you know, like we were committed and that was that and no turning back and soon enough it would all be over; but also really anxious. And for just a flash I felt squeamish again, like wrecking was somehow wrong. But sorry, it had to be done. Jeffrey Pratt, the enemy of my ally Theo, was a crud, plain and simple, a crud with glassy eyes.

■   ■   ■

The next day, my seventh day at Sherman, Theo met me quickly before first bell. He let me see the wrecker. It was wrapped in some loose-leaf. He had failed to catch Jeffrey on the way to school. He was going to try again, like we had planned, during second hour.

One thing, though, was worrying me. What if, after Jeffrey was wrecked, someone found the wrecker? After all, it'd just be lying there next to Jeffrey. Someone might figure out it was us who had done it. I mean, the wrecker would be evidence...

Theo scowled. "No it won't. No one'll know. It'll be done, burnt out, it'll only work once, I know it will. It'll just be a bunch of junk again, and no one will know who did it. You think anyone would think it was us? Who's gonna think two stupid kids like us could destroy the mind and soul of another kid?" I didn't know what people thought of me, but I knew Theo was considered very smart, not stupid at all; but by *stupid* he didn't mean *no brains*. The way he said stupid I could tell he meant *pathetic*, *cowardly*, *stepped-on*, *nobody*. Not too kind, sure, but not too wrong either.

Theo said, "Look, I'm not worried. So why are you? Don't worry, okay?" I told him okay. I wished him good luck.

And then we went to our morning classes.

■   ■   ■

Mr. Fusillade told us something interesting.

It had nothing to do with what we were studying, though. We were studying the Aztecs and the Spanish conquistadors, but that stuff seemed to bore Mr. Fusillade, who always went on about the Civil War instead. "The Civil War," he'd say, "that great and glorious, horrible time when the South tried to leave the country and the North fought them to keep them in. That war is history, my goblin youth"—I'm not sure why, but Mr. Fusillade always called us his goblins or goblin youth—"*real* history, not like this conquistador drivel." Oh, sure, that was a bad thing for a teacher to say about what he had to teach, *drivel*, I mean; but that's Mr. Fusillade for you.

"William Tecumseh Sherman!" he boomed. "And I mean Sherman the Civil War general, not Sherman the junior high school. Good ol' Doubleyoo Tee fought for the North, for the United States, for the Federal Government, for Honest Abe Lincoln himself." Mr. Fusillade raised his fist. "Ah, what a face Sherman had! You can just see the *war* in it. Hard, harsh, barbaric, it's all there, in his forehead, his wrinkles, his beard. A war face—as if the war had gotten into his look, like poison into a fruit."

As usual, Mr. Fusillade was marching up and down our rows as he rumbled through his story. If someone got out of line, like chatted with a neighbor or tried to do homework for English, he didn't even bother to stop his talking. He had a whole set of signs, you see, a hand this way, a scowl that way, that told us exactly what we were doing and what would happen to us if we kept it up. No kid messed with Mr. Fusillade more than once.

"The Civil War, my goblins, was *ferocious*, and Sherman, good ol' War Face himself, had a lot to do with making it that way. See, the rebels, the Southerners, believed that the new country they were making, the Confederate States of America, y'know, was strong and permanent; but Sherman was going to prove to them that it wasn't. He planned to wreck their new country *so bad* that they and their kids and their grandkids would never forget the destruction and never try to throw off the Federal Government of the United States ever again. So he took his army and marched it through Georgia and South Carolina and North Carolina, right through the heart of the South. His army destroyed cotton, cotton gins, barns, buildings, railroads, cattle, and anything they could pick up and smash. The homes along the way they just looted and defaced, and they left people begging for food. The Southerners couldn't stop Sherman's army. The heart of the South was ruined.

"Hey, Sherman didn't enjoy what he was doing. Some things just had to be done. He didn't love war. He didn't think it was romantic. After the war, long after, he'd go on speaking tours—he met so many people on these tours and shook so many hands that he started to lose the nail off his right pinky—and once when he spoke to a group of veterans—he called them *boys* 'cause they were his old buddies—he said to them—I've never forgotten this quote 'cause most people get it slightly wrong—he said to them: *There is many a boy here today who looks on war as all glory, but, boys, it is all hell.*"

That's what Mr. Fusillade told us. At the time I didn't make enough of it. Only later did it really sink in.

That was later, though. First came lunch.

By lunchtime Jeffrey still hadn't been wrecked. I knew this because I found the wrecker in my locker. I had left my locker unlocked, you see, and Theo had put the wrecker in there for me, just like we had planned. So it was my turn now. I stuffed the wrecker in the bag with my lunch—and trust me, it wasn't fizz that I felt in my gut: it was pure *oog*. But I had a job to do.

As usual I ate by myself. Actually I ate at the table with the other kids who ate by themselves, if you know what I mean. I didn't really mind, you know. I was used to eating alone in school. So I acted like normal: I ate my lunch, but the whole time I ate I was watching out for Jeffrey.

And then, between my peanut butter and jelly sand-wich and my Oreos—halfway through my lunch, that is—Jeffrey showed up. I mean *really* showed up. He ambushed me. Some soldier I was. Before I even knew what was happening, Jeffrey had sat himself down in the empty chair across from me. He sat with the chair turned around, its back at his chest. He sneered at me. I felt my heart scram-bling up my throat.

"So, froggy," he said, "why'd you snitch on me?"

His voice was full of snot. It was like a whiny growl. I had no idea what he was talking about. "Wha'whaddaya mean?"

"Don't act stupid, stupid. You snitched. You want I should kill you? I will. Fess up. You snitched."

With my heart around my throat I could only stut-ter, "Uh uh uh," and shake my head and shrug and look pitifully dumb.

"What a moron. The *knife*. You snitched about the knife."

What knife? Wait. Those kids in Mr. Bembo's class. Had that been Jeffrey's knife? He must have lent it to them. And then somebody told some teacher about it. Knives were against the rules, of course. Jeffrey must have found out who could've snitched—who, that is, had seen the knife. But I couldn't have known it was his! Why come after me?

Well, why not? I was still to blame.

Except I hadn't snitched.

Jeffrey rose over his chair, over the table, toward me like a lava flow, and scowled around his glassy eyes. His long blond hair hung down. He pointed his fist, his finger at me, like he wanted to dig out a fingerful of my flesh. He muttered low, "They found out it was mine. I got three points for that. One more point and I'll be suspended. And if I'm suspended you're dead. So fess up."

It seemed to me that if I confessed I'd be dead for sure. And I hadn't even *done* anything. It was his own fault, anyhow. It was his knife. *He* got caught. He deserved to be caught. He didn't have any right to bully me. He didn't have the right to bully anyone. Bullies have no rights. And then my heart let go of my throat and I got hot. Now I was mad. Jeffrey was close and ready to kill me. I knew I couldn't beat him if he started slugging, but I wasn't about to let him think he had the right.

Did I think to use the wrecker? No, I didn't.

Just as low as him I muttered, "I didn't tell on you. I did see some kids with a knife. I don't know if it was *your* knife. But I didn't tell on them, either."

I wasn't as brave as I sounded. My voice might even have cracked, maybe twice, although I don't know. I wanted to say something more, like insult him somehow, call him a scum, but I wasn't strong enough for that. All I did was say my piece and then await my death.

Jeffrey made a kind of face like a crying baby makes. He went *boo hoo hoo* and whined, "Ooh, the little sassy didn't tell on me. The little sassy didn't know whose knife it was." Then his face went hard again. He reached toward me. He flicked a finger at my forehead. The tip of his finger hit the skin on my skull like a BB from a gun. Man, did it hurt. Then Jeffrey said, "Liar," and went away.

I sat there with a pain thumping over my eyes.

I hated Jeffrey then. Completely hated him.

I didn't see Jeffrey again until after school. I went to Mr. Shoe's class with the wrecker still unused. Theo was upset. You can bet I *never* told him I had *completely* missed a perfect chance to wreck Jeffrey during lunch—no way I told Theo *that*; I just told him my mission had failed. Theo fumed. He didn't get mad at me, he just got mad, and he got in such a sour mood that when I tried to give him back the wrecker he snapped, "Keep it," like he didn't want to even *think* about the whole stupid, awful, rotten business anymore. So I kept the wrecker where it was, bulging in my pocket.

Yeah, Theo could be way too impatient, but I think you know that already. And sometimes he was too easily frustrated. But, you know, it *was* nearly the end of the day, and we still hadn't done Jeffrey in. He was getting away from us.

Mr. Shoe started class by going over our homework. One of the problems was hard, and Mandy didn't understand it even after Theo had shouted out the answer. (Theo may have been in a sour mood, but that didn't keep him from shouting out. His sourness made him all the louder, I think.) To help Mandy, Mr. Shoe gave her a simpler problem. She didn't answer right away. When she did, she got it wrong. Mr. Shoe said, "Well, that would be true if—" and he explained when Mandy's answer would've been true. "But here," he said, "think about this," and he wrote an equation on the board and pointed at one of its numbers and, after giving a couple of hints, waited for Mandy to think it through. That's how Mr. Shoe was in class. He waited for you to think it through—whenever he could, that is; whenever the class was calm enough to let him wait; whenever Theo was bored or busy and didn't call out the answer. Mandy said she didn't want to think it through. She said this in a hostile way. But Mr. Shoe stayed as nice as ever. He tried to help Mandy through the simpler problem. He calm-ly led her along. Then Mandy said it was stupid. I could hear Mr. Shoe getting kind of tired, worn out, but he finally gave up on Mandy only when Theo interrupted him again.

When we were done with the homework, Mr. Shoe said, "So" and clapped his hands once, the way people do when they don't quite know *what* to do besides say "So" and clap their hands. He said, "Ahhh-hm." Then he remembered what we were going to learn that day, and he started teaching us.

I didn't pay much attention. For the tenth time that hour, I remembered what had happened to me during lunch. I mean, I could hardly forget it. A rage at Jeffrey bubbled up inside me. Why hadn't I wrecked him when I'd had the chance? Not only had he been right in front of me, with no one else nearby, but I had been hot and mad enough to do him in without a thought for right or wrong. But what had I done instead? I had let him hurt me; that's all. I should've wrecked him. I should've clicked the wrecker on and tossed it across the table, bounced it, rolled it at Jeffrey's chest, and then jumped away—and it would've gone off, spraying its demon fires all over him, into him, *hiss* and *shoom* and *fwump* through his skin; and the fires would've torn throughout him, *skree* and roaring shrill like an army…

I remembered what Mr. Fusillade had told us about Sherman's march through the South, the way his army had destroyed what it could, and I saw Jeffrey filled with my army of demon fires while my face was shriveled with war. Terrible, yes, but *some things just had to be done.*

No glory in that, I know—

I didn't want to think about it.

To distract myself I looked out the windows. Nothing out there but the parking lot. I looked back in, at the walls. Those were almost bare. Mr. Shoe wasn't like Ms. Gasperwit, who covered every inch of brick. He had put up an assignments chart, but that was nothing much, and over the chalkboard were the only other things on his walls—the first ten counting numbers in Japanese. These were swishes, slashes, lines painted black on white cardboard pieces, with the sounds of their names written in English underneath: *ichi, ni, san, shi, go, roku, nana, hachi, kyu, juu.* One through ten. Mr. Shoe had told these to us, had even tried to teach them to us. He had learned Japanese in college, you see, before he was a teacher. He loved Japanese and wanted us to love it, too. But we didn't care. Like we'd ever use Japanese numbers to count. By the time I was part of his class, he was giving up on teaching them. He just left them on the wall unused. He never got around to taking them down.

I started counting to myself in Japanese. I'd never thought I'd ever count in Japanese, but now the numbers were tumbling in my head. I let them tumble. I distracted myself with the sounds of Japanese numbers: *ichi*, *ni*, *san*, *shi*, *HISS*, *go*, *roku*, *SHOOM*, *nana*, *FWUMP*, *hachi*, *kyu*, *juu*, *SKREE*… but the sounds of wrecking got mixed in.

And then I felt something warm in my pocket.

It was the wrecker.

It felt very warm, too warm. Like it was *on*. But it couldn't have been! Had I knocked the switch? Like bumped a desk against my leg and knocked the switch? I *must* have, *because the wrecker was on*, I felt it, it was way too completely *hot*… but I'd've been wrecked already if it were on, right? Something was wrong. I almost put my hand in my pocket to check the switch, but then I got afraid that *then* I'd knock the switch on and I'd be wrecked for sure. But maybe the wrecker was just, like, only overloading, sucking up the battery even though it wasn't on, and getting hotter and hotter until it'd simply blow up. No, no, I was nuts, it wasn't hot at all, not even warm, if anything was warm it was *me*, all oogy and sweating. Oh, the whole thing was just too dangerous. What were we doing? We were idiots! We hadn't thought it through. The wrecking of Jeffrey would be *horrible* and we'd get caught, I just *knew* it, they'd figure out it was us, yeah, they'd find our fingerprints on the wrecker—you can *bet* they would—and then it'd all be over for Theo and me.

But then a big part of me snarled at me and said that no matter what, it'd be worth it, because Jeffrey Pratt, like every other bully, deserved an awful wrecking.

Mr. Shoe finished his lesson, and now it was time to start our homework. Theo had already started, and like always he was doing the odds and not just the evens like we were supposed to. He was too busy to turn around and chat with me. During homework time that's how he was. Mr. Shoe walked around us, looking over our work, giving help, loaning pencils. "I'm always loaning pencils out," he said to one kid, "and no one ever returns them. But I'll find one for you. Let me see, let me see." Todd and Robby, and other kids, too, started goofing off, and Mr. Shoe tried to shut them down.

I stared at Mr. Shoe. Poor Mr. Shoe. He had no idea he had enemies. C'mon, teacher! Look at your kids. They don't respect you. They think you're a dope. Open your eyes, Mr. Shoe! But he wouldn't see. Kids stepped on him and he let them do it. No one, no grown-up, no kid, should ever be that way. You be that way and what do you get? Bullied, that's all.

I was annoyed. I was hot.

I decided to scold Mr. Shoe.

When he came around my desk to look over my work, I said to him, "Mr. Shoe, why do you let it get so noisy in here?"

I think I embarrassed him a little. He looked sadly around the room. He rubbed his face. He was very tired. He smiled for me, but not very well. "I don't mean to. Teaching's hard. You can't always set things up the way they should be. Not everybody listens to you all the time."

I could tell he was feeling sorry for himself. I felt sorry for him, too, but I figured he still deserved a scolding. So I asked him, "Mr. Shoe, do you have kids at home?"

He blinked at me. "No."

"Do you have a wife?"

"No."

"Do you have a girlfriend?"

"No. Why do you ask?"

"Do you have a dog?"

"No, I live alone."

"Well, then go find a mirror at home and yell at *yourself*. Practice being *mad* at someone. Get good at it and maybe people will listen to you. Okay?"

A laugh burst out of him. He looked at me with this happy kind of amazement. He didn't know what to say. He shook his head. "Tell you what, Michael. I'll try. Okay?"

I wasn't sure I could believe him. I think he got my

point, but he was too good-natured about it all. I guess that was kind of my fault. It was the way I'd put it, really—it was *funny* to him, even if he understood how serious I was. Oh, well. I said what I said. It was up to him to make something of it.

That was it: being mad at someone. Not just mad *because of* them, but *at* them, so they can see it, so they can know they make you mad…

After school, Theo and I hurried to catch Jeffrey on his way home. "Gimme the wrecker," Theo cried, as he hurried along. Oh, I tried to slow us down, if only to keep us from accidentally knocking the wrecker's switch and wrecking ourselves. I told Theo, "Wait," but it did no good. "Gimme it," he cried, as he snatched it out of my hands.

Then at the edge of a field, we saw Jeffrey. He saw us. He came at us, turned right around, happily ready to slug and sneer and stir our hate. Then I didn't care about right and wrong. I saw Theo's warface, I felt my own, and when we were close enough to Jeffrey, before he could even get in a fist or a violent word, Theo clicked the wrecker on and tossed it at him, surprising Jeffrey *and* me. Theo and I broke away, we scrambled to the left and the right, hoping we'd get far enough from the wrecker's power to survive.

Yeah, I was scared. No time to think, though. Theo had attacked and that was that. His impatience had thrown us into it at last, and we had to run for our lives.

As I was breaking away I saw Jeffrey flinch. Of course he hadn't expected us to throw some kind of grenade. For a flash he was even scared, I think. He didn't know, he couldn't know, what was going on. Over my shoulder, as I ran, I watched and heard what happened to him.

Zzzzzzzt. That was the wrecker going off.

Poompf. That was the fires escaping.

Klok. That was the wrecker hitting Jeffrey's face.

Thump. That was Jeffrey hitting the ground.

Sure enough, the wrecker had worked.

And I felt sick inside.

When it was clear that Jeffrey was down and not moving, Theo and I walked back, slowly at first. Then we ran. We stood on either side of Jeffrey. We were alone at the edge of the field, and alone we stared at what we had done.

So what does a person look like, someone who's been wrecked? A lot like Jeffrey did, I guess. He was flat as a board. His hands were stiff. His eyes went back and forth, *tic* toc *tic* toc *tic* toc *tic* toc, like all but the simplest parts of him had been completely shut down.

Jeffrey was really wrecked. He seemed that way. But how? I saw a red mark between his eyes, where his nose and forehead came together. That's where the wrecker had hit him. But it hadn't been the hit that had done him in; it had been the fires. Had it really been fires I saw? Or just some kind of spark? Have you ever put your finger right *there*—at the cross of your eyes, your forehead, and your nose—not touching the cross but getting so close to the center, and then felt a creepy kind of electricity, like a tiny electric bubble was rising out of your head? Sometimes it only works if it's someone else's finger. Maybe you've never even felt it, but I have.

I figured that the fires, the awful spark, had smeared with that kind of bubble. The bubble and spark had short-circuited, and Jeffrey's brain had fried. He couldn't move. He couldn't think. All in all, his mind was shattered.

I really felt sick again.

But what about his soul?

The soul isn't electric, is it? Souls are something else. If Theo's wrecker had really shattered Jeffrey's mind, then had it also burst his soul? I couldn't even imagine how. What are souls made of? How can you burst one?

Who would know how?

I looked up at Theo.

He wasn't dancing over Jeffrey's body. He was standing there like me. But there was a touch of fizz to his look, a crooked kind of smile. Theo knew how to burst a soul. Maybe he *didn't* know, I mean enough to explain it; but he could *do* it. Jeffrey, it seemed, was proof of that.

Was Theo Vee a kind of demon?

No, no way. He was just a *boy*. So okay, he was pushy, kind of obnoxious, often inconsiderate. He may not have been meek, but he wasn't *mean*. He never tried to hurt anyone. Yeah, yeah, yeah. He hurt Jeffrey. Hurt isn't the half of it. But who started all this? Theo was simply striking back. Of course his strike was pretty extreme. He had done an evil thing, I guess. So was he a demon? I had helped him, you know. Was I a demon, too? Or is that just an excuse? Boys, mere boys, can do evil things.

But can they *wreck?*

I wasn't just sick now. I was scared.

If we had *really* wrecked Jeffrey—and it looked like we had—it didn't matter how much I might go on about minds and souls and this and that. No matter how you cut it, Theo and I had *killed* Jeffrey Pratt.

His body was still alive, though.

I squatted down to see if it was breathing. It was, but it kind of had to be. I mean, the eyes were still going *tic* toc *tic* toc. I had heard that when you dream your eyes do exactly that, go back and forth, really fast. And *then!* what a hope I suddenly had! With any luck Jeffrey was just, like, *dreaming*, kind of zapped, knocked out in a really weird way.

"Theo," I whispered, "is he wrecked?"

Theo shrugged. "Looks that way."

"Maybe he's only knocked out."

"No, he's wrecked." Theo squatted down, too. He reached toward Jeffrey's face but didn't touch it. "It worked. The wrecker worked. My things always do." He pulled his arm back and stood up. "Good. Right. Um. I—" His voice cracked. He sounded unsure, unhappy, maybe even sick inside. Then his voice hardened again. "He deserved it. Let's go."

I put out my hands, palms up, over the body, like to say, *But we can't just leave him here.* "Are you sure he's—?"

Theo snapped, "Yes, I'm sure. And I'm glad. He's gone. We did it. I did it." He scanned the ground, found the wrecker, bent down, and picked it up. It was charred and melted. He nodded at it, satisfied. "Let's go."

"Theo, I—"

He calmly asked, "You ratting out on me?"

"No, but—"

"Then are you coming?"

"I'm not sure—"

"Never mind. You were a good ally."

Theo didn't say anything more. He was done. He looked at Jeffrey one last time and, without saying good-bye to me or see you later, he left.

I know I told you Theo wasn't mean. Normally, he wasn't. But Jeffrey had made Theo's murky anger into a crystal rage, all callous and cruel. And so Theo could simply walk away. If he was not a demon himself, some demon had a hold of him.

I didn't follow.

I stayed with Jeffrey. It's not that I felt sorry for him. In a lot of ways I still thought he deserved what he got. Sure, it was kind of hard to hate him now. I'm not the kind who kicks people when they're down. But I didn't feel sorry for him, not exactly. I stayed because I couldn't simply walk away. I felt too *guilty* to go.

I wanted so much to believe that Jeffrey was only in a terrible daze. He had to wake up sooner or later. He *had* to. Of course if he *did* wake up he might start hurting us again. No way I wanted that. So what could I do? As I stared at him I got an idea. Since his eyes were more or less working I figured his ears were too, and like he was kind of hypnotized and could take the suggestion, I said this to him:

"You can't slug Theo anymore. Me neither. Do you

see what we can do to you? Do you see now what our anger is like? Just leave us alone and we won't hurt you. Forget about us. Just go away. Don't bully us anymore."

Did he hear me? I could only hope. I decided to see if he might come out of his daze. I wasn't sure I wanted to touch him, but I finally lifted him by the shoulders, bent him at the waist, and got him to sit up. He didn't change. So was the wrecking permanent? Theo never said it *had* to be. We just assumed it would be. But was it?

Suddenly Jeffrey trembled. He shut his eyes, squeezed them shut, like he was squeezing out a pain. He lifted his hands and rubbed his cheeks. He opened his eyes, slowly, and looked at me. My heart skipped. "Who are you?" he mumbled. My heart sighed. "Nobody," I said, "I found you here. Are you okay?" Jeffrey shook me off and stood himself up. "Yeah, I'm okay." He looked around us, got dizzy, and almost fell. "I must've tripped." He stared at me, trying to place my face. He didn't know who I was. It was like I was wearing a mask. "I gotta get home," he said. He left.

I stood up and watched him stagger away.

I wasn't sure what the wrecker had really done to him. It had done *something*, that's for sure. Jeffrey didn't know who I was, he didn't attack me, he didn't insult me, he wasn't even rude to me. Maybe the wrecker had, after all, shattered a mind and burst a soul—but the mind and soul of the bully, not of the boy. A bully had been wrecked, and a boy was left behind in the ruins. And then maybe on top of everything else, the boy had taken my suggestion to leave Theo and me alone. But all of that would mean Jeffrey had been more than just a crud. He'd had something *human* in him. What was this, some kind of moral? Like, was someone saying to me and Theo that bullies are people, too? Forgive me for not believing this. I suppose it could be true, but it's not very easy to believe.

Then I realized that whatever had happened to Jeffrey Pratt, whatever the wrecker had done to him, he was different. He was *new*. And Theo was still the same. Even after we had won, his smile had been crooked. His rage stuck in him like a nail—and though he might finally heal around it, it would probably never go away....

Still, the bully was *gone*. Whether or not Theo's rage went away, it didn't have a point anymore. Without a point it would hurt him less and less, until someday, it couldn't hurt him at all.

And *then* Theo Vee would be new.

Theo freaked when Jeffrey showed up at school the next day. He caught me in the hall and was frantic. "You've got to be my ally again," he cried. "The wrecker didn't work!" I told him not to worry. "Wait and see what Jeffrey does."

Jeffrey did nothing.

He never did anything again. He didn't seem to recognize Theo or me. We passed him a few times in the hall. He didn't even sneer. He wasn't friendly, he wasn't polite, he wasn't suddenly full of sunshine. But he did leave us alone. In fact he left *everyone* alone. He was more or less a normal boy. I even heard some kids talking about how different Jeffrey was. It was just like I told you—the bully in Jeffrey was gone. Even Theo had to believe it. At first he thought he'd been cheated somehow—that *all* of Jeffrey should've been destroyed—but I convinced him that that wasn't necessary.

And so, finally, my alliance with Theo Vee was ended.

Did Theo and I become friends then? No. Theo had never wanted a friend. He thanked me for being his ally and that was that. *I* had wanted a friend, sure, but I let Theo go. I didn't try to keep him; I didn't think I should try. You see, when Theo told me he was glad I had helped him, he cried "We did it, we did it!" with *such* a grin, that I had to wonder if a demon still had him. I didn't think so, but it was hard to tell. Even when he was happy, Theo was usually a bit demonic, a bit too much out of this world. And I don't mean just the way he would act. There were still his Things, you know. Maybe Theo wasn't merely ingenious but had borrowed a bad magic from somewhere. Oh, I'm sure some scientist could have taken any one of Theo's Things and explained it perfectly. Then again, maybe only some evil sorcerer could have. Naw, that's kind of dumb. You know as well as I do that Theo's Things weren't the least bit evil—and neither was Theo. I'm not sure *what* he was, or if he was just a boy genius, but I'm sure he wasn't evil.

Even so, he scared me. Hey, I liked Theo, I really did, he was a lot like me, but I wasn't too sure I should be around him. He had pulled me into something I wasn't very proud of, you know. What kind of friends could we ever be with our spirits so alike? I mean, who would we be wrecking next?

I didn't want to find out.

Soon after all this, they put Theo in some special class, an experimental thing that mixed up sixth, seventh, and eighth graders, all of them too bright for their own good. Mr. Shoe agreed to this transfer. He, too, wanted Theo to have "a learning environment more suited to his needs." But I think Mr. Shoe, despite everything, was sorry to see Theo go.

Theo did okay in his new class, or so I heard. He was calmer. He almost fit in.

I didn't talk to Theo again. There was nothing for us to talk about. He went his way, I went mine. Yes, that meant I was pretty much left to myself, but I was used to that. I wasn't *too* sad. It's not like the world had completely ended. I still had the year ahead of me, after all. Theo Vee wasn't the only kid at Sherman, the only possible friend. Life went on.

So. Do you believe what happened with me and Theo? Some of you might think it's all a lie. No kid could build what Theo built; no one could. No one could wreck a bully's mind and soul. Is that what you're thinking? Well, go ahead and think it. Most of you, though, and especially *you*, know I'm telling the truth. It's really so simple. Once upon a time there were two boys and a bully. The boys got together and struck the bully down. The bully went away, and the boys got on with their lives. That's all that happened. Yeah, okay, so the details are a little weird. But weird is what makes it interesting, after all.